# The King's Ransom

B. Heather Mantler

Mantler Publishing Prince George

ISBN:0986875902
ISBN-13:9780986875908

LIBRARY AND ARCHIVES CANADA CATALOGUING IN
PUBLICATION


MANTLER, B. HEATHER, 1987-
THE KING'S RANSOM / B. HEATHER MANTLER.


ISBN 978-0-9868759-0-8


I. TITLE.


PS8626.A676K56 2011      C813'.6      C2011-906266-6

This book is dedicated to all those who believed that I could do this.

# KING ALDOUS IS CAPTURED BY KING CASIMIR

Aldous was glad when the guards finally removed his shackles and pushed him into the small cell. The cell was drafty and dark, but it was private. A luxury he had not had since the war began between his kingdom and Casimir's. Aldous knew that as a prisoner of war it was expected that he would be paraded out for the crowds, like any other royal prisoner. He was just happy that the parading was over and he didn't have to be on display for a while. Casimir might put Aldous put on trial for war crimes in the next week or so. Aldous would handle that with the dignity befitting a king, but, while in this cell, Aldous was relieved to be just another prisoner.

Aldous crossed the room to the far wall. He sat down on the stone floor and leaned against the stonewall. His feet burned and his lower back ached. Aldous still wore the armour he put on this morning when he prepared for battle. Now it felt three times its normal weight. Aldous removed the gloves and bracers. He placed them in a pile to his right before rubbing his wrists where the shackles had left them raw. Aldous was grateful that King

Casimir had taken his helmet as a trophy because Aldous was not confident he was strong enough at this moment to remove it himself. Aldous untied the knots holding his breastplate in place and removed the breastplate. He placed it on the floor beside his bracers and gloves.

Aldous knew that he would remain in this cell, the size of his closet, until his son, Garibold, paid the ransom that Casimir would demand for Aldous's return. He had raised his son the best that he knew how, but Aldous was not sure that Garibold was ready to rule the kingdom. He lacked the confidence and the maturity that was necessary for the job. No, Garibold would not be a good ruler until he was older. Some noble would probably step up as Garibold's advisor and Garibold would end up as a puppet. Garibold's friends lacked ambition and would probably not bother so it would have to be another noble. The kingdom did not lack nobles that were hungry for power and position. Even so, it was unlikely that Garibold would pay the ransom unless the people demanded it. Aldous had never been as popular as his father had been so he doubted that the people would demand anything. The identity of the king did not really matter to most of the residents of the kingdom unless the king was bringing in a lot of money for the people. Aldous had never been able to do that; he had never figured out how. His father had tried to tell him and Aldous had tried to listen, but the lesson had never stuck.

Aldous leaned his head back to rest it against the cold wall. His eyelids felt heavy so he gave in and let them close. But his mind would not let his exhaustion consume him; instead it insisted on replaying the events of the day over and over again in his head. Had he really been captured this morning? It felt like it was at least a week ago since he had woken up from the hour of sleep that he had gotten after spending most of the night planning the day's attacks.

*Brigham entered the tent and bowed to Aldous.*

"You requested to see me, my king," Brigham said.

"Are the men ready?" Aldous asked as he strapped on his right greave.

"And waiting, your majesty," Brigham answered, "Would you like me to send someone in to help with your armour?"

"No," Aldous answered, "It takes twice as long if I have help." Brigham was silent and did not move. "Does each leader have the attack instructions for today?"

"Yes, your majesty," Brigham answered, his tone suggesting disapproval. Aldous strapped on his left greave before reaching for the next piece of armour.

"Is there a problem?" Aldous asked.

"I do not mean to question you or the orders, but," Brigham stopped as if he was scared to finish his thoughts. Aldous made a face at the armour while his back was turned to Brigham. He had told his men that they could speak freely around him and to him, but they still were afraid that he would punish them for contradicting him. Aldous turned back to face Brigham as he put on the next piece of his armour.

"Speak," Aldous said, his tone a little sharper than he had intended.

"You will not have the necessary guard for your protection," Brigham finally spat out what he was trying to say.

"It is necessary if we are to carry out this plan of attack," Aldous said, "We have one advantage and I do not want to waste it."

"Yes, your majesty," Brigham said.

"I will be ready in a few minutes," Aldous said, "Have the first two squadrons gone by the time I get out there."

"Yes, your majesty," Brigham said. He bowed to Aldous before turning and leaving the tent. Aldous sighed as he picked up the next piece of his armour.

Aldous finished putting on his armour. He stopped and stood still for five minutes in mediation for the upcoming battle. He heard Brigham directing the first two squadrons to leave. After the five minutes Aldous reached for the medallion that hung around his neck and pulled it out. His father had given it to him when Aldous was ten. His father had told him that it was Saint Milon. Aldous did not know what realm Saint Milon controlled, but he hoped that it was protecting kings. Aldous kissed the medallion as he sent a prayer to Saint Milon asking that everything go well today. Then Aldous left his tent.

The last seven squadrons were waiting for him. One of the squires was holding the bridle of Aldous's horse. Aldous refused the offer of help and then climbed up on his horse.

"The next two squadrons need to get moving," Aldous announced to the waiting men. The next two squadrons separated themselves from the group and went in opposite directions. Everyone else settled in for a bit of a wait.

Aldous was double-checking his gloves when he noticed a shadow of a bird going over the area. He looked up. There was a black bird flying in the opposite direction from the battle. A shiver ran through the knights seated on their horses. Even the horses were a little skittish until the bird had disappeared from sight. The men did not say anything about the bird because of Aldous's presence. He knew that if he were not there they would be speculating as to whether it was a crow or a raven. A raven was good luck, but a crow was a bad omen. Aldous went back to checking his gloves and wrist bracers.

"I want the next two squadrons moving," Aldous said just as the men were starting to get antsy. This caught all the men by surprise, because the next two were suppose to move out when everyone else did. But the next two squadrons separated themselves and rode off.

The servants and squires were busy taking down the camp. They would meet up with the knights in the evening, when they would set the camp back up for tonight. Aldous had never seen much point in carrying and setting up this type of camp every day. However tradition stood that kings should have comfort wherever they travelled and that meant moving camp to where the king was. The knights seemed to appreciate the camp at the end of the day, so Aldous did not say anything about his preferences. There was no point in upsetting the men with him. Aldous knew that loyalty to the kingdom reached only so far before his men would just turn him over to the enemy. And he had already made them uncomfortable just by being in battle. Fortunately Aldous had managed to get out of the castle without twenty servants following him around and driving him insane. He had squashed the idea of anyone going with him on the basis that there were plenty already coming.

"Let us ride," Aldous shouted when enough time had elapsed since the last two squadrons had left. Aldous led one squadron straight towards where the battle would be, while the other squadrons went in separate directions from each other and to the right and left of Aldous. They had camped in a clearing in the forest so it was forest they were riding through to get to the field where the battle would take place.

Aldous felt better now that they were moving. Two knights rode slightly ahead of Aldous, one on each side of him and two more slightly behind. The camp was quickly out of sight and soon the sounds of it being taken down were also gone. The only sounds Aldous could hear were hoof beats on dirt road. The smell of horse mixed in with the scent of the forest. Aldous felt himself relaxing and enjoying the ride. Even the battle at the end of this ride seemed so far removed.

The light of the field was starting to show through the trees when an arrow came out of the woods and hit Brigham in the thigh. The squadron halted and everyone put themselves between Aldous and the danger they could not see. Slowly men came out of the woods. They had King Casimir's emblem on their chests, but the rest of their clothes were green. And there were enough of them to surround the group. Several were archers and stayed back in the trees. The ones coming out had swords in their hands. The obvious leader stopped in front of Aldous and the squadron. The leader had a cloak on so it was hard to tell what he looked like, but he was fairly tall. Aldous could see two brown eyes that said he would do whatever was needed to get what he wanted, but really hoped that it was not necessary.

Brigham looked like he was in pain from the arrow wound, but he had drawn his sword with the rest of the group. Somehow Aldous's vision changed and he could see the futures of the men around. Brigham had a son with him. Gar held two baby girls. Selwyn was twice as old as Aldous was now and holding his grandson while his son stood by and watched. Aldous knew that none of these men around him had wives. If there was anyway to prevent these men from dying today Aldous was determined to find it.

"What do you want?" Aldous demanded of the leader.

"King Aldous, whom you are," the leader answered with a grin. Aldous noticed that the leader had an extra piece as part of the emblem on his chest. No one would have noticed, but Aldous has seen Casimir's emblem a lot this last couple days.

"And you are?" Aldous asked.

"A servant to King Casimir," the leader answered, the grin getting wider, "We can do this without bloodshed or with a lot of bloodshed."

"And what are you proposing?" Aldous asked. The men around him did not like the sound of this and the tension in the air heightened.

"We take you all prisoner, of course," the leader answered, "You and your men just need to give up."

"I do not think that would work," Aldous said. Gar seemed to sigh with relief, but the rest of them were still tense.

"However, there is another alternative," Aldous said. The leader leaned on his sword and pondered this idea.

"I am listening," the leader said after a few minutes.

"I will come as your prisoner if you let my men go," Aldous said. The men around Aldous did not like this idea and a few of them grumbled.

"Sire," Brigham started. Aldous silenced him with a look and Brigham did not finish what he was going to say.

The leader thought this over as he studied the group of knights.

"I should try to take all of you prisoner," the leader said, "But I will take the deal you offer. You in exchange for letting your men go free."

"Head back to where camp was," Aldous's voice was the right volume for his men to hear, but no one else, "And do not look back. Now."

The squadron of men fell away from Aldous and started back toward camp. Aldous thought he saw Brigham glance back but it was hard to tell. Aldous stayed where he was. The leader and his men did not move. Finally the sound of horses died away and the leader gave a signal. The men went back into the trees and came back with horses. One of the men brought the leader his horse. They mounted their horses and surrounded Aldous on all sides before all of them started forward. Aldous directed his horse to stay in the group though the beast did not seem pleased at being a captive along with his master.

They rode out of the forest and across the field, where the battle had not started. The squadrons that Aldous had sent out first were already in position and the men stared as their king rode toward Casimir's capital city as a prisoner. Before the group was across the field each squadron had sent a man back to camp to find out whether the battle would continue or whether this counted as losing the war. Aldous wondered what Brigham would say. He might continue the war because he wished to get his king back, but Aldous hoped not. Or Brigham might send word back to Garibold and see what instructions he received before making a decision. Aldous hoped the Garibold would find some other way to deal with the situation.

The group reached the city and the second in command of the group took the lead through the streets. The leader disappeared around a bend and Aldous could not tell where he went. People looked up briefly when the group went passed, but went back to work. They did not recognize Aldous as the captured king because there had been no announcement. And these people seemed to have no interest in the war between kingdoms. Aldous saw many children out and running around along with women. The men were dressed as if it were another day at work. The only guards to be seen had been at the gates coming into the city, not in the city itself. Aldous knew that in his capital city every corner had a guard and women and children stayed inside because while the kingdom was at war it was better to not be out if the enemy invaded the city. Aldous's respect for Casimir increased. Any king that could keep a war being fought outside his gate between the kings and not involve the people was a good king. Aldous wished he could be as good a king.

The group escorted Aldous to the gates of the palace itself. The guards at the gates let the group through. In the courtyard the group stopped beside a stable where they dismounted. Aldous dismounted when the group did. He left his horse in the middle of the group as he followed the second in command, and was followed by some of the group, to the door of the palace. The door was twelve feet tall and had intricate designs carved into it. Casimir's crest was in the centre with a half on each door. The guards opened the doors and let the group in. The walls of this palace were stone painted a deep purple. The floors had been painted an emerald. The ceilings were twelve feet in height and were not painted, giving the palace an unfinished look. The hallway behind the door was long, straight and had no doors off of it until near the end. At the end of the hallway there were two seven-foot doors that went left and right and a ten-foot door that was exactly at the end of the hallway. There were two more guards in front of the ten-foot door. The group went toward the door and stopped just short of the guards.

"We are here to see his majesty, King Casimir," the second in command announced.

"The king will see you in a few minutes," the guard answered. Aldous and the group stood there and waited.

Finally there was a knock on the other side of the door. The guards opened both doors. The second in command waited in the hallway. Aldous could see the throne room. It was similar to his own with a large area for the court and a raised dais at the end. There were two main chairs on the dais with two chairs on a step down and behind. Only one of the chairs on the dais was taken. The chairs on either side were empty, as was the rest of the room. Apparently court was not in session today. The only one there was a man walking back across the floor. Aldous assumed that he had been the one to knock. The man bowed to King Casimir before taking the chair to the right and behind. After finishing taking in the white pillars and the deep purple and emerald silks on the walls Aldous turned his attention to the man sitting on the throne. He was maybe a year or two older than Garibold, which made Casimir about twenty. However he held himself up as a king should. His clothes matched the walls and the current season's fashion among the nobility. His brown hair was cut short and light enough that the gold crown almost blended in. He was clean-shaven, which might have made him seem younger than he was. Aldous guessed that elf blood ran in the royal line just as dwarf ran in his own family line.

The guards had the doors fully open now and one stayed inside while the other went back to his place.

"Tybalt and his warriors," the guard's voice boomed before the guard waved the group into the room. The group entered and stayed between two parallel black lines that were painted on the grey floor. They stopped at the black line that was a couple metres away from the throne. Everyone bowed when they stopped, even Aldous.

"Welcome," Casimir's voice was soft, "Who is this with you?"

*"Sire, this is King Aldous," Tybalt answered. Aldous looked up at Casimir and into very familiar brown eyes. A couple of guards came in one on the side doors.*

*"You may speak," Casimir said. Aldous realized that he had opened his mouth.*

*"I am here in exchange for my men being left alone," Aldous said.*

*"Very honourable of you," Casimir said, "Perhaps this could be the end of the war."*

*"I do not know if it is or not," Aldous said, "It depends on what is decided now that I am absent."*

*"I will send a message," Casimir said, "Saying that my men will not attack unless provoked."*

*"Thank you," Aldous said.*

*"The same message will contain the amount which I will require for me to release you," Casimir said.*

*"I expect as much," Aldous said.*

*"In the mean time you will stay in a cell in the tower," Casimir said. Aldous nodded.*

*"Sire," the man sitting in the chair to Casimir's right said.*

*"Yes?" Casimir asked. The man got up and walked the short distance to Casimir and spoke quietly in his ear. Casimir nodded and the man went back to his seat. Tybalt and his warriors had bowed and left the throne room. The guards that had come into the room came and put shackles on Aldous's wrists. They removed his weapons.*

Aldous felt the light come into the window of the room. He opened his eyes to see the rays of light coming through the barred window. They revealed the cell to be small, grey stone, and cold. The only things in the cell were some used straw that might have been used as a bed once in the corner and a bucket sitting beside it. Aldous stood up and looked out the window. He could see the city below. People were just starting to move around. Aldous could also see the city walls and beyond. The field he could see was the one in which he was suppose to fight a battle yesterday. Now he could see both sides were on their own edges of the field. It relieved Aldous that they were not fighting. Aldous reached into his shirt and took out the Saint Milon medallion. He kissed it as he sent a prayer up for the lacking of fighting before tucking it back into his shirt. Aldous sat back down beside the pile of armour and leaned against the wall.

The door to the cell opened and a guard stepped inside. He placed a bowl on the floor beside the door and then left the room, closing the door behind him. Aldous went over and picked up the bowl. It was oatmeal. Aldous ate all of it. Then he used the end of the spoon to mark a short line on the wall. Aldous put the bowl and spoon back where the guard had left it. Aldous took off the rest of his armour and piled it in the corner. He only had the tunic and pants that he had been wearing under it, but that was enough. Without much else to do, Aldous divided most of the rest of the day between watching people out the window and meditating.

Two guards came back at supper. One switched the bowl for a plate of food and the other took the bucket. Aldous ate and put the plate back. When the two guards came back one took the plate and the other left the bucket.
Aldous watched the sunset before curling up beside his armour and going to sleep.

On the seventh day marked on the wall with the handle of the spoon the door opened shortly after Aldous had finished breakfast. Casimir stepped into the cell. A guard was going to follow him inside but Casimir shook his head at the guard. The guard stayed outside, but only closed the door half way. Casimir looked around before getting within arm's length of where Aldous was sitting. Casimir held a scroll in his right hand.

"I sent a message to your men," Casimir said.

"I saw that there was no more fighting," Aldous said.

"Your son send back a message," Casimir said, "And he said he had no interest in further battles."

"I am glad he made that choice," Aldous said.

"The city of Tiregous is now part of my kingdom," Casimir said, "And your men have gone home."

Aldous nodded.

"I have your son's reply here," Casimir held up the scroll, "I thought it better that you read it yourself." Aldous accepted the scroll and opened it. Casimir took one step back, but remained in the room.

*King Casimir of Lithimin,*

*I, Crown Prince Garibold of Proster, am willing to accept defeat in the battle for the city of Tiregous. The city now belongs to you and is part of your kingdom. The knights will be withdrawn by a fortnight.*

*As to the matter of my father, King Aldous, according to the laws of the kingdom of Proster I cannot pay the ranson you ask for. I cannot pay any money or order someone else to pay the ransom. As much as I would like to have my father back I find I have no other choice but to leave him at your mercy. I wish there was some other arrangement that could be made to have him returned, but I fear those might also go against the laws of this kingdom.*

*Crown Prince Garibold*

Aldous rolled the scroll up and offered it back to Casimir. Casimir stepped forward to take it back.

"And what is to happen now?" Aldous asked Casimir.

"You will stay in this cell as my guest," Casimir answered, "I can not provide furniture, but I can provide bedding and anything else you need within certain limitations."

"Bedding, a change of clothes, parchment, a quill, and ink," Aldous said, "That is all I want, all that I need."

"They will be delivered," Casimir said.

"Thank you," Aldous said, "For you kindness and mercy."

"My father did not believe in doing more harm than necessary," Casimir replied.

"How did we ever start fighting in the first place?" Aldous asked.

"I killed my diplomat," Casimir answered, "when I found out that he was taking money from one of your nobles to pass along false messages. I learned of the true messages when he decided to cleanse his soul of any wrongdoing before he died. If I had known the true messages there never would have been fighting between us."

"Did he feel the need to tell you which noble?" Aldous asked.

"No, I am sorry," Casimir answered.

"How did You, Tybalt and the warriors know where I was riding?" Aldous asked.

"A man named Jarlath," Casimir answered, "He gave no other method of identifying himself than his name."

"Lord Jarlath," Aldous said, "is a power hungry noble from within my court. I had been warned that he was devious, but I did not think he would stoop to the low of giving me up to the enemy."

"Perhaps he was the one paying my diplomat," Casimir said.

"I would believe that of him," Aldous said, "now that I know what he has done."

"I will have what you have asked for sent to you," Casimir said. He gave a slight bow from the waist before leaving the room. The guard closed the door behind him.

An hour later Aldous received an old mattress with bedding along with writing implements, a book of blank pages, and a note saying the clothes would be along in the next few days. The guards cleaned up the straw in the corner and took the pile away before putting the mattress there. By the time supper arrived, Aldous had his cell set up in the way he wanted it.

# WHAT KING ALDOUS DID WHILE SITTING IN KING CASIMIR'S PRISON

The dawn of the morning after Aldous received the writing materials he sat down below the barred window and set everything up around him. Finally he opened the book to the first page. Aldous dipped the quill into the ink and gently touched it to the paper.

*The History of Proster as told by King Aldous the sixth in line after the invasion and destruction of the Batend army.*

Aldous studied his work for a few minutes. His writing was much neater than during his years as a student. Perhaps time without writing for hours every day helped one's hand. Aldous smiled briefly to himself before dipping his quill in the ink again and putting it on the page.

*Proster was named after King Proster, who was the seventh son of King Thedious of Grankle, after King Proster took over the country next to Grankle. No one has ever been found that remembers the name of the country before that. King Proster was proud of himself and his warriors in their ability to take over a whole country. He named himself king. He named each of warriors a lord and gave them a piece of land to rule over.*

King Proster ruled with an iron fist. He felt it was better to be feared than respected. He showed no weakness, or any emotion at all. A few of the peasants spread stories that he was an evil wizard's golem. King Proster did nothing about the story when he heard it. It is believed by many historians that he had seen so many battles that he had blocked out all of his emotions. Even some of his warriors were scared of him and what he would do to them if they did not obey his every command. King Proster ruled for ten years in this way.

However, it was in this tenth year that King Proster changed. He caught sight of a peasant's daughter in the market place. Though she was covered in dirt and wearing rags King Proster fell in love with her. He had her brought to the castle. Her father went with her because he was scared of what would happen to her. If she was dishonoured he would never be able to marry her off and he was willing to stand up to King Proster if necessary. Rather than be angry with the father, King Proster welcomed both into his throne room. There were only two guards in the throne room with them. King Proster came down off his throne to talk with this man and his daughter. King Proster told the truth and laid his heart out on the floor of the throne room. He told them about how he closed his heart after his mother died because he was always afraid that it would get hurt again. He was sure that no one in the world was worth that kind of pain. But seeing the woman in the market place the casting around his heart had cracked and fallen away. He had fallen in the love with the woman and nothing in the world meant more to him at that moment than her. And then King Proster asked both father and daughter for the daughter's hand in marriage.

The woman saw in King Proster's eyes that he told the truth and fell in love with him at that moment. The father did not agree until he saw that his daughter had fallen in love and was willing to marry the king. The father accepted the marriage. King Proster made the father a lord and gave him an estate that was currently without a lord.

The plans for the wedding began immediately. The wedding would take place exactly a week from the moment that the father had agreed to the marriage. People found that King Proster was often distracted during that time as well as merciful. Rumours abounded about a witch had cast a spell over King Proster and his heart. Even when the invitation was sent out that *everyone in the capital city and anyone that could be in the capital city by the time of the wedding were invited to attend there were still many rumours.*

Aldous stopped writing and wiped off his quill before putting it down. He gave the page a few minutes to dry before closing it. Aldous put the book to one side before standing up to stretch. The guard opened the door. He switched the bowl for a plate of supper while the other guard removed the bucket from the room. Aldous went over and picked up the plate. He ate the food. Then he put the plate back. Aldous was standing at the window when the guards came back. Once the cell door was locked behind the two guards, Aldous went to bed.

The next morning, Aldous was woken by the guard bringing breakfast. Aldous ate the food in the bowl, marked one day on the wall, left both bowl and spoon by the door, and sat down in the spot he had sat in yesterday. He picked up the book and opened it to the page he had left off. He opened the ink and dipped the quill in to it. Aldous touched the quill to the paper.

*King Proster married his bride and both were happy. After that King Proster showed emotion and no longer ruled without mercy. The kingdom prospered under the rulership of King Proster and his new approach to life. Every prisoner in the dungeon was given a new trial. Many of them were let out as having served the right amount of time for the action they committed against the crown. Others were let go with compensation for being locked up for minor crimes that should have only been given a fine as punishment. Trade with neighbouring kingdoms was suddenly encouraged. Beggars and orphans were given homes in places that King Proster ordered to be built. The orphans were taken care of by some priestesses from a church that was growing in popularity in the kingdom. King Proster did not have a church built for this religion though the priests and priestesses repeatedly asked for one; however, he did nothing to stop another nobleman for paying for a church to be built. The religion became the unofficial one of the kingdom as more and more of the population became members. King Proster never worshipped any gods in public. He did wear a medallion to Saint Ingram, which is the saint of good luck and fortune. This medallion was to be believed to have been given to him by his fighting instructor when he was ten-years-old.*

This also fits with the stories that King Proster always refused to participate in any kind of religious ceremony as Saint Ingram is said to have the one imperfection of jealousy. King Proster did not stop his wife from participating, as was her belief.

There are many stories from King Proster's reign, before and after his marriage. The most famous story being the story about the horse trader. The horse trader had arrived in the city as he had hoped to sell some of his horses at the faire that would be taking place outside the capital city for a week shortly after harvest. The horse trader left his merchandise with his partner in stable they had rented for the week. He had arranged for them to have an area at the faire to display some of their horses and see how many they could sell. Not uncommon since that was mostly what the faire was for, people buying and selling goods now that they knew how much money they had and how many supplies they had for the winter. This horse trader decided that he could afford a few nights in the city and rented a room at a fairly high priced inn that was owned by a nobleman's third son. The first one had married young, had children and was prepared to take over for their father. And the second had married a girl from a neighbouring kingdom. The third was given a choice as to what he wanted to do so he decided to marry the daughter of the inn owner down the street and inherit that business. It turned out that he was good at it. The horse trader paid for his room, dropped off his belongings in his room and asked directions to the nearest brothel. The horse trader never got to the brothel because he was distracted by a beautiful woman right there in the inn. However this woman refused his attentions. So the horse trader went back up to his room for the night. He dreamed of the woman that night. The next day at the faire he took the time between customers to find a booth of a potion maker. He bought a love potion and took it back to the inn with him. He put a couple drops into a drink that he had seen the woman taking sips out of and muttered the incantation that the potion seller had taught him that was suppose to make sure that she would fall for him and not just the first man she saw. That night the horse trader got what he wanted. The potion seller had told the horse trader the incantation to make the effects of the potion disappear, but the horse trader, knowing that he would be in town for several more days, decided not to make the effects go away any sooner than the morning he had to leave. In the middle of the night *the horse trader was waken up by several city guards breaking down the door to his room. The woman was sleeping beside him and he was naked as he sat up and blinked at the guards. The guards ordered him to get out of bed. The horse trader climbed out of bed. The guards allowed the woman to wrap the blanket around herself and leave the room. The horse trader was thrown his pants before the guards made him gather his belongings and march out of the inn. He was given a cell in the dungeon for the night and the next morning was taken before King Proster. In the throne room along with the king and guards was the woman the horse trader had drugged, a man in the garb of an innkeeper, and a man in the clothing of a nobleman. Apparently the woman was the innkeeper's wife, which most people hearing the story guessed the moment the horse trader laid eyes on her. However what the horse trader did not know was that it was the innkeeper's drink that his wife had been stealing sips out of that night. After feeling a strange attraction to one of his customers the innkeeper found himself disgusted at the thoughts that were coming into his head about another man and then saw how the man was looking at his wife. From that he figured out what happened. The innkeeper wanted the effects of the potion removed from both him and his wife, and then wanted the horse trader to compensate him for making his wife unfaithful, to which the city guard could testify. King Proster had softened up a lot from his marriage and so he made the horse trader give up all the money he and his partner made during the faire as well as all the money the horse trader had with him. The horse trader was forced to say the incantation to get rid of the effects of the love potion. And then King Proster gave him fifty lashes before having the guards leave him outside the city with the threat of death if he ever showed his face there again.*

Aldous was disturbed by the guards that brought supper and took the bucket. Aldous wiped off the end of the quill and let the page dry before closing everything up. Then he ate the supper that was left for him. He had finished and set the plate down when he heard the door being unlocked. He moved back to his corner before the door opened. Once the guards had come and gone, he went to bed.

The next morning when his breakfast was brought, so was the change of clothes he had asked for. The guard also brought in a pitcher of water. Aldous ate breakfast first. Then he washed up before changing his clothes. He washed his clothes in the remaining water and had spread them out to dry. Only once he had finished that did he sit back down under the window and get his writing supplies ready.

*King Proster and his wife had three children. Their names were Zebulon, Hertha, and Narda. Hertha married a nobleman from the kingdom of Grankle. Neither she nor her children returned to Proster. Narda disappeared the day after she turned fourteen. No one saw or heard anything of her again. There are no rumours as to what happened to this very popular princess. No stories among the nobles or the peasants have lasted beyond that time or there were none to tell. She may have died and Proster refused to have it written into any history books, but this theory is doubtful as she disappears from all history oral or written from all surrounding kingdoms as well as Proster. If she had died and her fate taken from the history books it would have only been the history books from Proster, not neighbouring kingdoms as well. And there is also the possibility that her name would have been completely removed from the history books instead of just her fate.*

*Zebulon married the daughter of one of King Proster's warriors. He gained the throne when his father died from pneumonia after a very hard winter. Zebulon's rein was quiet time in the kingdom. There was no battles, no attempts to take over the kingdom, or any changes to the economic condition of the country. In fact the only story from Zebulon's rein is of the two con men that showed up at the castle gates one rainy night. They claimed that they could play music so beautiful that the listener could only hear the beauty as reflected from within themselves. Zebulon let the two men play as he and his court ate supper. With one man on the lute and the other on the horn they played during supper. They were the worst musicians Zebulon had ever heard, but everyone else was sure that they could hear the wonderful music that the men claimed to play. After supper the nobles of the court excused themselves with various reasons that made sense only when viewed through the fact that many believed that the fact that they could not hear the beautiful notes was due to their own failure. Zebulon let each noble leave as he sat there all evening listening to the music. Many nobles believed that King*

*Zebulon must have heard the beautiful notes that the men claimed to play. King Zebulon made the men play half into the night, even when they tried to stop because of tiredness from travelling all day. Finally King Zebulon let the men stop. He gave the men the scraps from supper that were not given to the dogs and then let them stay in the guard's shed outside the walls. He also had the guards destroy the musical instruments once the men were asleep so that they could not try to con anyone else.*

*The only other piece of information necessary to know from King Zebulon's rein was that he only had one child because once his wife gave birth to the boy she refused to sleep with Zebulon and took on lovers from the squires and stable boys that were around the castle. She gave birth to three more children, but Zebulon denied any of them power in his kingdom. All three grew up as servants in the castle and were never told who their mother was, nor is there any record of which servants were her children. All that was recorded was the fact that she had three children out of wedlock and the children became, as their fathers were, servants in the castle. Zebulon's wife died in childbirth of her fifth child. However neither she nor the child survived.*

Aldous cleaned the quill while he waited for the page to dry. He carefully put both away just before the guards came in for their first evening visit. Once the door was closed Aldous ate the food on the plate before putting it back. He was at the window watching the sunset when the guards returned. Aldous stood there until the last ray of light had disappeared from the sky. Then he got into his bed and drifted off the sleep.

Something disturbed Aldous's sleep causing him to open his eyes and look around. There was nothing strange or different in the room. Aldous sat up when he thought he heard the sound for a second time. Concentrating Aldous listened to see if the sound would come again so that he could pin point where it was coming from. It was silent, aside from the usual night noises, for so long that Aldous started to lie down again. The noise came again. It sounded like someone had moaned.

"Who is there?" Aldous demanded. Slowly a transparent person appeared in the centre of the room. The ghost was a woman. She had long flowing hair that in life had been black, eyes that appeared to be the same light blue as in life, and a white burial gown fit for a queen. Aldous stared at the ghost of his dead wife, Theola.

"Am I dead?" Aldous asked once he could get his jaw to work again.

"No," Theola answered, there was laughter in her voice, "Saint Milon thought you might be in need of some company and asked me if I would like to visit you. Something you did pleased Saint Milon, because he usually does not do favours for his patrons. Of course, I was not going to turn down his offer to see my husband. Even in death I worry about you and how you are faring and whether or not you are taking care of yourself. I worry about Gari as well, but as one of the resting dead I cannot just visit anyone without special permission. I am glad to get a chance to see you. I suppose, now that you are here in a cell belonging to King Casimir, Gari is now on the throne of Proster. He will be a fair king, not a great king, but a fair one."

Aldous had settled himself back on the bed and listened to his wife talk. It was so much like when she was still alive that Aldous smiled to himself.

"He was such a good boy growing up. I loved to watch him as he went about his life. When I died, I wanted to stay longer because I knew that I was going to miss watching him grow up and into his role as king. Even through he will only ever be a fair king, Gari would look so handsome in that crown. I hope he finds the right woman to rule at his side, but the wrong woman would tear him to pieces. And with his good looks I am sure he would have the wrong ones clamouring for his attention and he would be flattered by it. Probably so much that he would miss the right woman when she showed up. Back when we got married I thought we were perfect for each other. And we were for all those years that we were together, but with my death I am sure you must be lonely for companionship. If you ever meet a woman that is worth your love then I encourage you to marry the woman, because you deserve better than to be lonely for the rest of your life."

Aldous shook his head slightly. He knew that there was no other woman out there for him. Theola had been his soul mate.

"That is if you ever get out of this cell, but I'm sure that will happen. If you do not think of something then I am sure something will come along that removes you from this cell and lets you back into the world. In the meantime it is nice that you finally have time to start that book you always talked about writing."

Aldous must have fallen asleep because he opened his eyes and the sun was shining in through the bars. The guard unlocked the door and left his breakfast in its usual place by the door. Aldous got up and ate. He marked the wall before putting the bowl and spoon back. Then he sat down under the window and opened the book to where he left off. He dipped the quill in the ink and started writing.

*Zebulon abdicated the throne to his son, Driscoll, when an illness overcame Zebulon's body. Zebulon lived two painful years after he had given up his throne. Driscoll went to Zebulon many times in those two years for advice and counsel. It is recorded that when Zebulon died Driscoll locked himself in his chambers for three days while the rest of the kingdom went into mourning. They held the funeral while Driscoll was still locked away in his rooms because the law was that the body had to be buried before the night on the second day after the person had died. The only person Driscoll would allow into his rooms was a serving girl.*

*At the end of three days Driscoll came out and resumed his throne. There was nothing said about his absence or his father's death. The serving girl was sent to an estate that the crown held in the countryside. A year later Driscoll accepted a treaty with Menano that included marrying the princess. The royal wedding was held the day after the treaty was signed. It was a small ceremony for a royal wedding with only those at court in attendance. Nine months later the princess gave birth to twins, one boy and one girl. The nobles at court celebrated the birth, but Driscoll seemed withdrawn through* the birth and from the twins. He made his yearly three-day trip to the country estate during this time.

Rumours started to go around that King Driscoll was not right in the head and that was the problem. Driscoll was fair with his people, abrupt with the nobles, and rude to his wife through out many years of his life. According to one story Driscoll held court one day because there was a case between a nobleman and a peasant that could not be settled any other way. Driscoll sat and listen to the nobleman complain that the peasant's work wasn't done correctly. The peasant's response to all of this was that he did the best that he could with the pain in his knees, which had been caused by the nobleman when the nobleman kicked the peasant for being lazy once when he was a boy. Driscoll thought for several minutes when both sides were done. Then he looked at the nobleman and the peasant. He told the nobleman that he was stripped of his land, money, title, and owned the new owner of those every gold piece that he had spent in his life. Then Driscoll turned to the peasant and bestowed on him the title, land and money he just took for the nobleman. Driscoll ordered guards to accompany the men back to make sure his orders were carried out. Oribel, the princess Driscoll married, told Driscoll that what he had done to the poor nobleman was horrible. Driscoll turned to Oribel and told her to keep her thoughts to herself unless they were relevant to her knowledge, which was more useful in the bedroom than the throne room.

As far as anyone could tell the only person he spoke to like that was Oribel. Which confused people and many thought that their king was not right in the head. However by the time the nobles decided that something should be done about Driscoll it was brought up that neither of the now sixteen-year-old twins looked or acted anything like Driscoll. Both had darker colouring than Oribel and Driscoll and hazel eyes. Oribel had green eyes and Driscoll had blue eyes. They also were tall and thin, which in the royal line did not happen. King Proster had been the son of a half dwarf half human and a human. All of that line were stocky and on the shorter side. A few of the nobles remembered the half wild elf guard that had accompanied the princess when she had been brought to the kingdom. He had left a week after the wedding. Rana and Weldon looked like they were his children *instead of Driscoll's. The nobles chose to leave Driscoll alone about his behaviour towards Oribel.*

Aldous wiped off the quill and put away the writing implements as he waited for the ink to finish drying so that he could close the book. He put the book to one side just as the guards arrived. Once the door was closed behind the guards, Aldous ate his supper. Then he waited at the window for them to come back for the last time for the day before going to bed. Aldous's sleep was not interrupted by anything.

The next morning Aldous went back to his writing after breakfast. He continued to write the history of Proster. He only interrupted his writing for two things. On the second day of every week he was brought a pitcher of water with which he washed himself and one set of his clothes. And on the night of the fourth day of the week Theola visited him for a couple of hours. Sometimes they would talk and sometimes he would just sit and listen to her. And life continued that way. Once a year Aldous would receive a new set of clothing and when he finished filling a book he would ask for another one. Aldous worked on the history until it was finished to the end of the war he had started with King Casimir.

*On Driscoll's fortieth birthday it was decided that the day after the party would be a good time to announce who would be heir to the throne. The nobles wondered whether Driscoll would name Rana or Weldon or whether he would name the next nobleman in line. Driscoll, despite his attitude towards Oribel, had been a father to Rana and Weldon and raised them as if they had been his own, so many thought that Weldon would be given the throne even without being of the ruling line of Proster. Driscoll's birthday was a great celebration. All the people had been given the day off from work and invited to a banquet in the king's honour. Driscoll had several servants come from a neighbouring kingdom to serve so that his own could participate in the feast. Since Driscoll's reign had been prosperous, the party would not cause any money troubles, but every person that was at the feast went home with a belly full and a plate or two of leftovers.*

The next afternoon everyone returned to the castle for the announcement as to who would be the ruler after Driscoll stepped down or died. Driscoll's address to the crowd has been written verbatim in many history texts due to how important the announcement had been at the time. Though I am sure that the scribes wrote the words and were ready to move on to the next thing before anyone truly understood what had been said. There was nothing recorded as a response to the announcement, because the crowd was in shock and had no idea what to respond until after the scribes had packed up and gotten inside before it started to rain. Driscoll announced that Weldon and Rana would be given the titles of Duke and Duchess and given the roles of advisor to the king since both were well versed in court politics. But it would be Driscoll's own son, Hillel, who would become king. Hillel was a year older than the twins and rumours came in to light about a serving girl who many felt was not old enough to bear anyone children at the time when she worked in the castle. Though many now understood Driscoll's lonely trips to his estate in the country.

After that announcement Hillel moved in to the castle. It was so that he could get used to the castle, but also to let the residents of the castle get used to him. Weldon and Rana, according to all stories that have been found, were willing to let Hillel have the title of king while they sat on each side of him as advisors. Perhaps they understood that they were not blood of the Proster royal line and should be grateful for anything they received. Oribel had died three years before Driscoll's fortieth birthday. She had started to wander the castle lost in her own head, and sometimes with tears running down her face. Until one morning she was found dead on the cobblestones of the courtyard at the bottom of the tower. No one believed it to be anyone's fault but Oribel's own.

Hillel was very similar to his father in looks and mannerisms, but quite different in personality. Where Driscoll would be quiet, Hillel would be talkative. Where Driscoll slept alone, Hillel took any willing female to bed with him. Where Driscoll might yell if he got angry, Hillel would get violent. Hillel had the confidence that it took to be king. He was also well liked, with the exception of times when he was angry with someone. Hillel was also married when he arrived at the castle. His wife, Arabella, was a nobleman's daughter, who had met Hillel one day while Hillel was out riding and had left the property against the rules set for him. Hillel kept finding ways to leave the property on a regular basis to see her after that. They had fallen in love when they were too young to be together, but refused to let anyone pull them apart. The nobleman did not like the unknown boy that held his daughter's heart, but he found there was little he could do so when she was old enough he allowed her to marry the boy. The nobleman was happy to here the announcement about Hillel going to become king and his own daughter moving in to the castle.

On Driscoll's forty-fifth birthday, Driscoll went hunting with a party of nobles and a handful of his guards. The nobles and the guards returned without Driscoll. No one recorded what happened to Driscoll because none that returned would speak of the incident, which caused Driscoll not to come back. Nor would they speak to the question of whether he was dead or alive. Instead they said that Hillel was now king. A monument was erected in Driscoll's honour instead of a funeral. His date of birth was written at his feet, but the date of death was left as a question mark.

Hillel's reign started out with the announcement that Arabella was pregnant. While the kingdom waited for the birth to happen Hillel went out and started a war with the kingdom of Grankle, Proster's brother kingdom. Arabella lost the child. Hillel claimed that a spy from Grankle had poisoned a drink given to Arabella and it had caused her to lose the child. Word from the servants was that Arabella had begged her husband to stop the fighting and had poisoned herself when he was unwilling to do so. It was said after that Arabella was kept under guard and locked up at all times. She was given only what she needed and the only time there were no guards around her was at night when she was with Hillel. Within the year Arabella was pregnant again and Hillel was starting to gain ground in Grankle.

Hillel went in to battle with his men about a month before Arabella was due to give birth. He believed himself to have enough time to win more ground and be back in time for the birth of his child. The day Arabella gave birth to her son was the day that Hillel was captured by King Florian of Grankle's men. Hillel was decapitated the next day with multiple war crimes read out against him. The news of Hillel's death came to Arabella moments before she was going to make an attempt to kill herself to be away *from the man she had loved and now viewed as a monster. Duke Weldon stepped up as leader of Proster, since Arabella was not in any condition to rule as queen and her son was only a day old.*

*Weldon stopped the war against Grankle the moment he had received word that he was ruler. Hillel had not bothered taking anyone's advice when he started his war. Weldon also gave all ground that Hillel had taken from Grankle back to Grankle. He also compensated Grankle for their losses from the battle. And he paid the ransom to bring the knights home to their families. Weldon started Proster back on the road to prosperity that Driscoll had started it on and Hillel had detoured off.*

*Weldon also took on helping to raise Arabella's son, Waldemar. Waldemar would always consider Weldon to be his father, though Weldon had married a noblewoman and had children of his own. Arabella was happy to be free from Hillel and refused any help with her son, except Weldon's help. Waldemar was raised along side the son of Arabella's handmaiden. The boy would be Waldemar's companion growing up and his personal servant when both had grown up. I can still remember Father referring to the man as a friend instead of a servant, even at times when the man saw that it was inappropriate. Not that appropriateness stopped Father from doing anything he wanted when he wanted. Father claimed that as king he could do what he wanted as long as it did not interfere with the prosperity of the kingdom or the lives of the people. And it was other people that had to adhere to appropriateness, not him.*

*When Waldemar turned nineteen he was crowned king and Weldon went back to being a duke and an advisor. A year after that the peasants held a birthday party for him, which he attended and thanked everyone by giving them gifts rather than the other way around. The only thing he had kept that he had received as a gift was crown of flowers a small girl had made for him. The wizard had cast an everlast spell on it to keep it just as it was the day he had been given it. Every birthday after that Waldemar wore the crown of flowers instead of the royal crown because the crown of flowers meant more to him.*

*From the time that Waldemar turned sixteen offers of marriage had been coming from kingdoms all over the world. Most Waldemar turned down after meeting the potential bride. All were princesses and all would rather walk the walls of the castle with him where they could see the city than walk the streets of the city with him. Waldemar felt passionately about the people of the kingdom and despite being king he felt no need to lord over the people. At twenty-five Waldemar had stopped even looking at the portraits that were still being sent to him. He had come to believe that there was no woman out there that had the values he did and without them he had no interest in the woman. Madra was the daughter of a lesser nobleman from Grankle, who had sent her to Proster as part of group of other nobles because her father had no use for his third daughter. His third daughter spent time helping the servants with their work or went into the village and spent the day with the people as if they were her equals. The nobleman had forced her into dresses proper to her station and sent her to court with instructions that she was not to associate with those under her. Her guardian at court had no idea what to do with her after the fourth time in a week that she was caught disobeying her father's directions, so he sent her with this group of nobles. Waldemar watched this new group of nobles from Grankle arrive, knowing that the women were hoping to catch a young handsome king. Waldemar was trying to figure out how to avoid all the members of this party, except when having to be in his throne room, when he noticed the last woman of the group. She was dressed in the appropriate dress for a lesser noble, but her dress was dirty as the rest of the group was spotless. This intrigued him and he decided to find out more about the incident that dirtied her dress, because it did not look like it could have been caused by clumsiness. He asked one of the servants with the group, who he could get alone without being seen by the rest of the group. The servant told him about how she had helped a farmer in the market with loading his wagon and playing with his young daughter. The servant also related how horrified the rest of the party had been at this behaviour. That night Waldemar introduced himself to Madra. The day after they went for a walk on the city streets. Madra was impressed with this nobleman that was willing to stand at her side on a dirty street and help a woman with six children running around. It was only the next day when the group was introduced in court that she learned that the nobleman was none other than the king that all the rest of the women in the party were hoping to marry.*

On the day before the group of nobles were suppose to go back to Grankle they were in court again. All the ladies were wearing their best dresses in hopes that the king would notice them today even though he had not noticed them before this time. However Waldemar was late for court that day. Weldon had done the job as king until Waldemar finally arrived. Waldemar's silk outfit was covered with dirt and dust to the shock of all the visiting nobles, those who were of the court merely pretended not to notice. Rather than going to his throne and taking charge Waldemar instead pulled Madra out of the crowd and got out down on one knee in front of her and proposed. He listed not his love for her as one of the reasons for asking, but her love for the people and her acceptance of people as equals. Madra could not say no, for she had fallen in love with Waldemar and wanted nothing more than to marry him. The group of nobles were sent back along with a message to her father. Waldemar and Madra were married the day her father arrived and gave his blessing to the union. And the kingdom celebrated for two weeks.

To the joy of all Madra gave birth to a baby girl nine months after the wedding. Valda was a happy little girl and brought a smile to the lips of all who she came across. A year later Madra gave birth to a boy. They decided to call the boy Aldous. Most assumed that Aldous would be raised to be king and Valda would marry one of the neighbouring kings to keep the peace that had held Proster since Hillel's death. Waldemar and Madra felt that both children would be raised as if they may have to take the throne. And this continued when the third one was born when Aldous was three. For each royal birth the population of Proster celebrated. Even when the fourth and fifth arrived. It was however the sixth pregnancy that brought sadness. Madra gave birth to twins, but there was some complications with the birth. Madra died after she was given the chance to hold both children. The smaller of the two children went with her into the after life. A statue of Madra and the child was carved and placed in the castle garden. When the second twin died two months later due to poor health that stemmed from the birth, a statue of that child was also added to what was already in the garden.

Waldemar suffered from grief at the loss of his wife and last two children, but he found the will to keep going from the five children that required his constant attention. The youngest was a year and the oldest was seven. He raised us as he had started to raise us, as responsible children with values that mirrored his own.

Weldon had died when Aldous was four leaving only Rana as advisor to the throne. Rana was determined that Waldemar should get married again because she felt he couldn't handle five children by himself, even with servants helping in caring for the children, and running a kingdom. Waldemar did not want to remarry. And according to the stories from the people most felt that him remarrying would desecrate the memory of Queen Madra. Madra had always believed in soul mates and that one soul was not truly gone to the afterlife until the other joined it. Waldemar won the fight against Rana and remained without a new wife.

Valda and Aldous were raised as if either could have taken the throne. The three other children of Waldemar and Madra were raised to follow whatever path their lives took them. When Valda turned sixteen many offers of marriage arrived for her. Waldemar let her make her own choice, though he told her that he would not allow her to marry any of them until she was nineteen. One of her suitors was a prince of Yester, which is a kingdom on an island in the middle of an ocean. Or so the maps say. There are supposed to be great ships that take people from the kingdom at the shore to the island of Yester. I have seen a fisherman on a boat that was on a lake, but even at my age I still do not understand how a ship weighing so much could possibly float on water. I have also never seen an ocean, perhaps it has some difference over a lake that would help me understand. The prince from Yester arrived in court rather than send his portrait. Valda decided that she loved this prince, but she did not want to choose him without seeing how he lived and whether he had enough similar values in common with her. Father allowed her to go visit Yester as long as she took a few guards and a couple servants to escort her. The journey to the ocean went without incident and the word came back that they had boarded the ship. A month later Father received the message that the ship had been found smashed on some rocks and there had not been any survivors to find. Waldemar added a statue of his oldest daughter to the one of his wife and youngest children and Aldous was declared heir to the throne.

*When Aldous was twenty-three Waldemar became sick. Aldous was crowned king and his father was put on bed rest by the royal physician. The fourth day that Waldemar was sick and in bed he started talking to Madra. He could see her and she was waiting for him to join her so that their souls could go to the afterlife together. It is unclear as to how much of this was delusions from the fever and how much was Waldemar really talking to his wife's soul. By the end of the week Waldemar's soul had joined his wife's soul and the kingdom went into mourning. Aldous had left the black banners up until they were tattered enough that they had to come down. The people appreciated that from the stories that were heard by the king in his study. Aldous also added Waldemar's statue to the one of his wife and children. And there they stand in the garden. A monument also appeared in the centre square of the city dedicated to Waldemar and Madra's memory. Unfortunately all the peace and prosperity was broken by Aldous, who did not seem to have his father's way with the people. Aldous married the princess of Grankle, Theola, shortly after Waldemar's death. They produced a son, Garibold, within their first year of marriage. Theola died when the boy was ten. The first war since Hillel died was started over a village that sits on the border of Proster and Lithimin and the gold mine beneath it. The war ended when Aldous had a vision of what the future awaited his men if this war was stopped before it went any farther. Garibold now holds the throne as the crown prince of Proster.*

Aldous put the last period in place before wiping off his quill. When the ink was dry he closed the book. He placed it beside the pile of armour that sat in the corner of the cell on top of the first book he had filled. When the guards arrived with supper Aldous requested another book of blank paper. It arrived three days later. Aldous took this fresh book and wrote down everything he had learned about Saint Milon from Theola during her visits.

## PRINCE GARBOLD HAS RESTARTED THE FIGHTING AND WHAT KING CASIMIR IS GOING TO DO ABOUT HIM

On the day Aldous put the one-thousand, eight-hundred and twenty-sixth mark on the wall with the handle of the spoon, the door opened shortly after he had finished breakfast and had put both bowl and spoon back beside the door. The door opened and Casimir stepped inside the cell. The guard started to follow, but Casimir waved him to stay out. The guard did not follow Casimir into the cell. Casimir closed the door to the cell before turning to Aldous. Aldous took a moment to study Casimir and Casimir gave him the time as he looked around the room. Aldous noticed that Casimir's face held more lines than it used to and some of the brown hair now gleamed silver. In the five years that Aldous had been sitting in this cell, Casimir had aged about ten years, which was strange for someone of mixed elven blood. They must have been difficult years for Casimir.

"I need your help," Casimir said, skipping the formalities.

"I am not sure how much help I can be," Aldous answered as he wiped off his quill and put it to one side, "Perhaps if you tell me that the problem is, I will see what I can do."

"Your son, Garibold, has declared war on this kingdom," Casimir said, "My diplomat tells me that Garibold has been amassing an army since he sent the message five years ago to stop the last war between our kingdoms. He took over the kingdom of Grackle without much of a fight after a show of force. My kingdom is next and I cannot let him have it without a fight, but I cannot win a fight against that kind of force."

"And what help do you believe I can provide for this situation?" Aldous asked.

"Talk to Garibold," Casimir answered, "Make him see reason and peace. There is no reason for this war except the corrupt need for power."

"I do not know the present situation within Proster," Aldous said, "Which means I am unfamiliar with Garibold's reasoning for the need to conquer others. I would have see the situation before I could take steps to stop it."

"I will have to talk it over with my advisor," Casimir said, "I will bring you word of my decision soon." Casimir turned around and went back to the door. He opened it and stepped outside. The door closed behind him and it was locked from outside. Aldous picked up his quill, dipped it in the ink and started to write from where he had been interrupted.

Aldous wrote until it was close to time for supper. He wiped off his quill and put the writing implements away before closing the book and putting it away as well. The guards came in. One switched the bowl for a plate of food and the other picked up the bucket. They left. Aldous got up and got the plate. He ate the food off of it before putting it back. Then he went to the window and looked out. The camps that he had been seeing for the last week were sitting across the field from the city walls. Aldous doubted that Garibold was in one of those camps giving orders to the men and trying to make them feel comfortable around him. No, Garibold would still be in Proster sleeping in his own bed in the castle. He had never been one to get his hands dirty.

Aldous took out the Saint Milon medallion that hung around his neck. He kissed it as he sent up a prayer that Garibold would hesitate long enough in attacking Casimir that someone could talk him out of the madness. Saint Milon was the saint of peace and Aldous knew that he would get an answer.

The guards came back. One took the plate while the other brought back the bucket. Aldous wondered if they would be sent off to fight Garibold's men if the war did start and who would take their place.

When the sun's light was just finished disappearing, Aldous got into bed. He expected Theola to come and visit him as she had been doing for five years. He sat there and leaned against the cold wall. Aldous found himself very tired. He kept drifting off to sleep and waking himself up when he realized that he was asleep. Theola had not appeared. Aldous finally heard the watch being changed down in the courtyard. For some reason Theola did not come tonight. Aldous drifted off to sleep slumped against the wall.

In the morning Aldous was woken by the guard bringing him breakfast. Aldous ate and then marked the wall. Though counting the days had long ago started to seem pointless he could not bring himself to stop. He had to know how much time had past while he was outside the world. Aldous set the bowl back near the door and sat down under the window. He opened the book to the first page. His eyes slowly went over the words as he went through each page. Finally, in the late afternoon, he reached the point in the book where he had stopped writing the night before. The book talked about Saint Milon, who he was and what he stood for. It was just about finished. Aldous just had to finish summarizing his thoughts and beliefs on the subject of Saint Milon and then the book would be finished. Aldous set up the ink and took the quill out. He carefully dipped the quill in the ink and started the next paragraph.

The guards did not interrupt him when they entered and then left again. Aldous kept writing. The guard's return did not stop the flowing of words on the page. Nothing seemed to stop the words until the light started to fade. Then Aldous wiped off the quill and put the writing implements away. He put the book away once the ink was finished drying. Then he looked around. The guards had left the plate of uneaten food. Aldous picked it up and ate the cold supper. When he was done he placed the plate back on the floor and got into bed. Nothing seemed to be able to keep Aldous's eyes open and he drifted off to sleep.

Aldous woke up to the first rays of sunlight coming in through the bars. He crawled out of bed and went to the window. He looked out. The camps were still at a distance. There had been no change. Aldous was relieved as he sat down. He opened the book to where he had left off and took out the writing supplies. Aldous went back to his work.

He stopped to eat breakfast after the guard came in and switched the empty plate for a bowl of food. Then he went back to writing.

Aldous finally finished and was wiping down the quill for the last time when he heard a key in the lock. Aldous placed the quill and other writing supplies away as the door opened. A man stepped in to the room. The guard closed the door half way once the man was inside. After closing the book Aldous looked up and studied the man. He was taller than Casimir was. His blonde hair hid the white that was starting to make an appearance. He too had more lines on his face than his age dictated. He was probably a year or two older than Casimir.

"I am King Casimir's advisor," the man said, "My name is Alden. King Casimir send me to talk to you about the situation between Lithimin and Proster."

"I can see from here that Garibold has not ordered his men to attack," Aldous said.

"King Casimir has Prince Garibold talking about negotiating a treaty between the two kingdoms," Alden said, "He believes that he can stall Garibold's plans for Lithimin's destruction for about two months."

"As long as Garibold is willing to go along," Aldous said.

"Garibold has gotten confident in his ability to crush whomever he chooses," Alden said, "He will play along for two months before he gets bored and orders his men to attack."

"And in the two months?" Aldous asked.

"King Casimir hopes that you can find out the situation in Proster and then talk your son out of destroying Lithimin," Alden answered.

"Am I just being let out?" Aldous asked.

"There is a law in Lithimin that says prisoners that have been in prison for five years can have some time in court to plead their case again," Alden answered, "Tomorrow you will be brought to court and will plead your case without mentioning Garibold or the possibility of war. King Casimir will pardon you and let you go free. From there a man will help you get back to Proster. He will know you by the name Ralston and he does not know your story. I would suggest telling him as little of it as possible. He will take you to the gates of the capital city in Proster. After that you are on your own. King Casimir will try to send someone to let you know what plans are in place when King Casimir has figured them out. From that point we will have to discuss what to do next."

"What about the diplomat from Proster?" Aldous asked.

"Was called home yesterday and left this morning," Alden answered, "But King Casimir and I believe that there might still be a spy from Proster at court and thus we want to be careful about who knows our plans."

"I understand," Aldous said.

"Good," Alden said before turning towards the door.

"I wonder if you could do something for me," Aldous said as Alden put his hand on the handle of the door. Alden turned back to Aldous.

"What is it?" Alden asked.

"Give this to King Casimir," Aldous held out the book he had just finished.

"What is it?" Alden said as he crossed the room to where Aldous was sitting.

"Hopefully an understanding," Aldous answered as Alden took the book from him.

"I will give this to King Casimir," Alden said before turning and going back to the door. He left the small cell and the door closed behind him. Aldous looked around the cell. He had the writing supplies, but they were useless now that he was without paper to write on. He had his three volumes, two of history and one of Saint Milon, also his pile of armour that was starting to rust at the edges, and a pile of worn out bedding on a mattress that would hold up for the next prisoner. Aldous stood up and looked out. The camps were exactly where they had been the last time he looked.

Aldous knew that he could not just go to the castle and be taken in by Garibold. No, he would have to go in as a peasant and learn what was going on from the bottom. Not that looking like a peasant was going to be hard, Aldous mused. He knew without a mirror that he had grown a full beard. He could see enough of it to know that it was white with streaks of grey in it. His hair was also longer and whiter than it had been when he was locked up in this cell. He had developed a hunch from sitting and writing for all these years. And his clothes were thread bare enough that they would need to be replaced soon if he had been staying here. All he needed was a bag for his books and armour then he could be another traveling peasant. Aldous doubted that any of the knights would recognize him and take him to the palace, but he would have to be careful of that. He would have to keep his head down and not look people straight in the eye as he was used to doing. It could all work...maybe.

Aldous was still staring out the window when the guards came in to leave him supper. He ate and left the plate in its proper place as he had done for the last five years. He was back to looking out the window when the guards came back. He continued to stand there when they had left. It was a beautiful view and Aldous was going to miss it. When the sun's light had finally disappeared behind the horizon, Aldous crawled in to his bed. He thought he heard Theola whisper for him to be careful as he drifted off to sleep.

Aldous woke to the light of the sun coming in the window. He stretched, but did not move from the bed. A few minutes later the guard came in. He placed a bowl on the floor as well as a pitcher of water. Then the guard left. Aldous got out of bed and went over to the bowl. He picked it up and went to the window to look outside while he ate. The camps were in the same place as yesterday. When Aldous was finished eating, he placed the bowl back. This morning he did not mark the wall to show what day it was. He used the water in the pitcher to wash up and get himself somewhat presentable. Then Aldous sat down in his spot under the window and meditated.

It was slightly after noon when the door opened. Two guards entered. These were not the usual guards. These two had weapons and dress uniforms. Aldous stood up. The one guard put shackles on Aldous before they escorted him out of the small cell. Very little had changed in the palace, Aldous noted as they went through the hallway and down the stairs. They went through another hallway at the bottom of the stairs and finally reached a door that Aldous remembered led into the throne room. The guards waited for a cue. Finally it came and they led Aldous into the throne room. The throne had not changed in five years. The same colour silks were hanging on the walls. The dais had two thrones, and two chairs to each side of the thrones.

Casimir sat on one throne, while Alden sat in the chair to his right. A few nobles stood around the room this time. Aldous knew that Casimir needed the audience for this plan, otherwise this talk would be done as the last one in the throne room was done. The guards brought Aldous to the appropriate line. Aldous bowed in the proper way a king would in another king's court.

"You asked for a second look at your case, King Aldous?" Casimir asked.

"Yes," Aldous answered, "By your laws I am allowed that right having been here for five years."

"You are," Casimir said, "The charges against you are those given to a captured king during a war. Since this is just a review of the case and not another trial I ask not for your defence but for your redemption."

"I have spent five years going over the history of my line as well as the teachings of my governing saint, Saint Milon," Aldous said, "I had forgotten that my father would have never gone to war for any reason and I find it dishonourable to his memory that I did. Saint Milon is the saint of peace. I am sure that he thought of abandoning me to my animal nature when I declared war, but instead he had me captured without getting hurt so that I could sit and contemplate my foolish decision before he threw me to the wolves. On my father's honour and on oath to Saint Milon, I give my word that my days of starting wars are forever behind me. I have learned that my life's course is now set in a different direction and I hope you will let Saint Milon take me in that direction, which is why I stand before you today with the request that you review my case. I willingly accept what ever fate you choose for me."

Casimir sat looking thoughtful for several minutes. The court was silent, waiting to hear what would be Aldous's fate. Casimir continued looking thoughtful for several minutes after it would have been appropriate for him to say something. Alden started to squirm in the silence, as did the rest of the court. Aldous just stood still waiting without looking like the wait was longer than it should be. The guard's shifting armour seemed to bring Casimir out of his thoughtfulness. Casimir looked at Aldous.

"I pardon you for your crimes against the kingdom of Lithimin," Casimir said, "I am sure Saint Milon will hold your oath to be true. It is only through it that I let you go free. I have heard many others give similar speeches, but none were willing to give an oath to their governing saint. You are free to go." The guards removed the shackles.

"Thank you, King Casimir," Aldous said, "Before I go I have a favour to ask." Casimir frowned, as did Alden.

"I have granted you a pardon, what else is there that you need?" Casimir asked.

"I only ask for a cloth sack to carry my books with me," Aldous answered, "Nothing more."

"The guards will provide you with a sack to take your books anywhere of your choosing," Casimir said.

"Thank you," Aldous said before bowing. The guards escorted him out of the throne room. They took him back to the tower cell. A cloth sack was brought to Aldous. Aldous placed the armour into the bag first and then the books. He carefully tied off the top and slung it over his shoulder before following the guards out of the cell. They led the way down through the hallways. Finally they stopped at a door. One of the guards opened it. Then the two guards waited. Aldous stepped out of the door and out into sunlight. He closed his eyes and turned his face towards it. The door was closed behind him. Aldous did not care. Finally he opened his eyes and looked around. The door was around the corner from the big door that he had been taken in the first time he arrived. He was standing in the courtyard. Aldous headed for the large gates that led out into the city itself. The guards did not look at Aldous twice as he went through. They seemed to assume he was any other peasant that the king let free. Aldous smiled to himself, he would be perfect as a peasant when he arrived in the capital of Proster.

The city was not crowded with people, but there were many going about their daily business. None paid Aldous much mind. Aldous looked around, but did not see anyone who was waiting for him to take him back to Proster. So he started for the nearest city gate. The tower had faced this direction so Aldous knew the city as someone who had studied a map would know the city. He only managed to make one wrong turn. It was into an alley, where several bandits were sitting in wait. But the bandits merely looked at him and told him to move on. They had claimed that alley and did not need any beggars using it. Aldous turned around and went back to the main street. He went down to the next cross street and was back on his way.

He finally found the city gate that he was looking for. This was the closest gate to the road that would take him to Proster. The guards were starting to close the gates, but let him through with a warning that they would not let him back in tonight and not to cut it so close next time. Outside the wall there were several camps of beggars, gypsies and travellers. Once outside of those camps, it was just field. Across the field were more camps, but those were of Garibold's men waiting for the order to attack. Aldous stood where he was as the gates closed with an echoing thud. He was not sure what he would do next. As of yet there had been no one to meet him.

Making up his mind Aldous went over to the closest fire. It was a gypsy camp and they welcomed him into their circle. He was given a seat and a plate of food. Then he was left alone. The gypsies stayed up until the moon was overhead, then each one went to their wagons and to their beds. Aldous kept sitting there as the fires and candles around him went out. Finally there were only the noises of the night. Aldous got up. But before he could do anything, the gate to the city opened with a creak. A man drove a wagon out the gate before the gate was closed again. The man stopped the wagon and looked around. Aldous left the circle of the wagons and went over to the man. The man saw him and studied him.

"Your name?" the man asked once Aldous was close enough that he could use a hushed voice.

"Ralston," Aldous answered.

"I am your ride to Proster," the man said, "Get up on the back of the wagon."

"Thank you," Aldous said. He went over and got into the back of the wagon and set his sack down beside the boards that filled the back of the wagon. The man got the wagon moving. He headed for the woods on the other side of the field.

"I would suggest that you have a good reason for going to Proster," the man said, "Otherwise they will turn you away. And if you argue with them you will be stripped, beaten and left beside the side of the road. I have seen it happen before. I have my reason in the back, but you are merely a traveller that I picked up."

"My only reason for going to Proster is because my daughter is sick after giving birth," Aldous said, "My reason for going at night is because I was thrown out of Proster years ago. I hoped that I have changed enough that they will let me through so that I may see my grandson."

"Good luck to you," the driver turned back to where the horses were going. They did not speak as they travelled into the night.

They went passed the camps of Garibold's men. Although there were watches out no one bothered the wagon or the two men in it. Once in the woods the driver stuck to the road through the trees. Aldous drifted off to sleep despite the bumps.

Something jarred Aldous out of sleep. He blinked around at his surroundings to see what had happened. Another large bump came before Aldous figured out that it was exposed tree roots that the wagon was going over. The man had turned off the road and was going through a break in the trees to get to the main roadway. The wagon went over the last root with a thump and then over the grassy area before the wheels touched the roadway.

The man pointed the horses in the direction of the capital city and they went along the road. It was still night so there were no other travellers on the road, though Aldous could see camp sites at the side of the road.

Before long something strange came into sight. Three guards were standing in the road. They appeared to be guarding the road, not just standing there. The man driving the wagon started to slow down so that the horses would stop in front of the guards. Aldous did not recognize any of the guards, so he hoped that they would not recognize him. When the wagon was stopped in front of them one guard stepped forward.

"What is your business?" the guard demanded.

"Delivering wood," the driver answered. The guard nodded before turning to the back of the wagon. He saw the wood and nodded again before turning to Aldous.

"What is your business?" the guard demanded.

"My daughter is sick and I am going to visit her," Aldous answered.

"Sick with what?" the guard asked.

"According to the messenger she gave birth to my grandson and is not recovering from it," Aldous answered. The guard nodded and then went back to the other guards. He spoke to one for a minute. The driver waited patiently as did Aldous. The guards seemed to be waiting for either of them to act suspicious. Finally the guards stepped out of the way and waved the wagon through. The driver got the horses moving and the wagon continued on its course. The driver relaxed a little once the guards were out of sight around a bend in the road.

"It that normal?" Aldous asked.

"On every road into the capital city," the driver answered, "I'll have to go through one more of them before I get to where I am dropping off my load."

"Why go so far for wood?" Aldous asked.

"Crown prince Garibold will not let them cut down trees that close to the city," the driver answered, "The local nobleman made a deal with someone in Lithimin to provide the village with trees, but I expect that to dry up when Prince Garibold officially declares war on Lithimin. I would advise you to be careful who you talk to and about what. It could land you in a Proster prison without anyone hearing about you again."

"I will keep that in mind," Aldous said. The driver did not answer and the conversation stopped.

Several twists and turns in the road as well as a village brought the wagon to the front gates of the capital city. The sun was starting to rise and it lit up the stone wall that surrounded the city and the large wooden doors that were gates to the city. They looked exactly as they had when Aldous had ridden out of them five years ago on his way to war. The door was closed for the night. There were a few camps around the walls of people who had gotten to the gates too late. The people in the camps were starting to stir and pack up. The wagon stopped at the place where the path forked. One direction went straight to the gate and other direction went off to someplace else. Aldous picked up his bag and got down off the wagon.

"Good luck," the driver said with a nod.

"You too," Aldous replied. The wagon started moving and Aldous turned towards the gates. The wooden doors were starting to open. Aldous started up the path. He arrived at the gates as soon as they were fully open. One of the guards waved at him impatiently to go through when Aldous hesitated a moment before entering the city. Aldous started forward.

# KING ALDOUS MAKES FRIENDS AND AVOIDS GETTING INTO TROUBLE

The city did not look like it had changed much to Aldous as he wandered the streets. The buildings were the same. How people were starting their day looked the same. The only things Aldous could really see that were different were the number of guards walking the streets and the fact that there used to be more children playing in the streets. Aldous found it sad that there were fewer children seen. It felt like everything was trapped and could not get out when there were fewer children out playing.

After wandering the city a while Aldous found himself standing at the gate to the courtyard. The gate was closed and there were guards standing on either side. They watching Aldous as if they expected him to attack them and try to batter the door down. Aldous turned and went down a different street. He came to the market square. There were lots of venders, but few people and fewer beggars. Aldous bought breakfast from one vender, whose meat pies smelled delicious. The vender was happy to make a sale, even if he doubted that Aldous had money when

Aldous first stopped at his cart. Aldous took the meat pie and continued around the square until he came to a vender selling drinks. Aldous bought a mug of cider to go with his meat pie. Then he sat down on the low wall near the cider vender to eat. He had finished the meat pie and was drinking the last of the cider when two guards started toward him from across the market place. They did not look happy that he was sitting on the wall. Aldous stood up and returned the mug to the cider vender.

"Best to run," the cider vender whispered to Aldous as he accepted the mug back, "They will arrest you for loitering."

"Thank you," Aldous said as he checked where the guards were. They were only half way across the market place. Aldous headed for the nearest alleyway. He glanced back to see the guards were running towards him now. Aldous went into the alleyway and started to run. The other side of the alleyway was a street with various businesses. Aldous slowed down to a walk and turned left. He could just hear the guards entering the alleyway. Aldous walked down the street as if he was any other person. Until he came to a bakery, then he stepped inside and closed the door behind him. There were several customers ahead of him so Aldous waited patiently in line. He glanced out the window a few minutes later to see the guards run passed.

The baker had gotten through most of the customers; only one person was ahead of Aldous. Aldous studied the baker as he waited to be served. The baker looked familiar. Then Aldous realized that the baker used to be the castle baker. Aldous had gone down to compliment him many times for the delicious baking that the man had done. His name was Odoric. Aldous remembered him as a good-natured man. Odoric dealt with the customer ahead of Aldous. Aldous stepped forward.

"What do you need?" Odoric asked as he put the money away and was not looking at Aldous.

"A loaf of the best bread in the kingdom," Aldous answered. Odoric looked up at him. A smiled appeared on Odoric's face.

"Your majesty," Odoric said.

"Ralston," Aldous shook his head, "I do not want Garibold to know that I am here yet."

"Of course, Ralston," Odoric said, "A lot has changed since you left."

"I am already finding that out," Aldous said, "Two guards chased me out of the market place for loitering."

"If you had been caught you would have been taken to Prince Garibold and he would have given you a choice, you could go to prison or join his army," Odoric said, "It is a sad state of things."

"Why did you leave the castle kitchens?" Aldous asked.

"Practically everyone who worked under you was thrown out of the castle after you were captured," Odoric answered, "A few who were still young are all that is left. I opened this bakery before I could be taken into the army that Prince Garibold started building. Many were not so lucky. Now those that are young make and clean everything. And what they cannot make is bought here, which means that the food sellers have to make more than they are used to fill the need coming from the castle. And anyone without any obvious way to make income is drafted in to the army. The butcher down the street lost one of his apprentices that way. The boy was out with another boy and they were in the market place when a sweep was done and they were taken in to the army."

"I will have to be careful then," Aldous said, "Because that is the last thing I want."

"Will you do anything about the situation?" Odoric asked.

"Yes," Aldous answered, "But not right now. I need help and it will come, but it might take up to a month. Until then I will be around trying to find out anything I can."

"Of course," Odoric said. He wrapped up a loaf of bread for Aldous. Aldous glanced outside; there were no guards in sight.

"Where are the children?" Aldous asked.

"Inside," Odoric answered, "Except when their parents cannot keep them there. Boys as young as ten have been taken in to the army and girls have disappeared completely."

"That is horrible," Aldous's voice was soft. He turned back to Odoric.

"I would appreciated if you kept my presence to yourself," Aldous said, "It is better for me that way."

"I will. Here is your bread," Odoric said holding out the wrapped up loaf of bread. Aldous accepted the bread and put it in his bag before digging in to his pouch.

"Save your coins," Odoric said, "It pleases my heart to see you again and that is enough payment for today."

"Thank you," Aldous said. He started for the door. He opened it and checked outside. The guards were coming out of a shop down the street. Aldous stepped back inside the bakery and closed the door.

"You can get out the back," Odoric said as he lifted a piece of counter to open the way. Aldous went through the opening and Odoric put the counter back. Odoric led the way into the kitchen as Aldous followed. Odoric went passed by everything to a door that was at the back of the kitchen. He unlocked it and opened it for Aldous. It led to an alleyway. Aldous stepped outside. Odoric closed the door and Aldous heard it lock. Aldous checked both directions before heading in the direction of the shop the guards had come out of. He passed the back doors to many other shops until he finally came to an open street. There were no guards in sight as he stepped out. He headed down the street towards the city wall.

Aldous was far more careful of guards as he went than he had been this morning. He finally found himself in the part of town where poorer residents lived. The buildings were more run down than they had been five years ago. Aldous found an alley with a small amount of shelter from a half collapsed building beside it. Aldous sat down on some stones and set his bag down beside him. He sat there and thought about everything he had heard and seen this morning.

Aldous's thinking was interrupted by a sound near him. Aldous looked over and saw a pair of eyes looking out at him. Aldous smiled at the eyes.

"Hello?" Aldous said. The eyes came out of the shadows enough that Aldous could see that they belonged to a boy. The boy was probably about six and was skinny with only rags for clothing.

"Hello," the boy's voice was hushed.

"I am Ralston," Aldous said, "What is your name?"

"Jasper," the boy answered.

"Do you live around here, Jasper?" Aldous asked.

"A few houses down," Jasper answered.

"Do your parents live there as well?" Aldous asked.

"No," Jasper answered, "They are dead, I live with the lady that lived next door to us when my parents were alive."

"Is she nice to live with?" Aldous asked.

"She tries," Jasper answered, "But she has to work hard to feed us all."

"How many of you are there?" Aldous asked.

"Me, Leander, Leander's sister, Ruby, Honora, Durand and his brother," Jasper answered.

"That is a lot of people living in one house," Aldous said.

"We have enough space," Jasper replied. He came completely out of the shadows and sat down on a rock near Aldous. "It is just hard to get enough food to eat."

"Are you hungry?" Aldous asked.

"Yes," Jasper answered. Aldous opened his sack and pulled out the wrapped up loaf of bread. He gently peeled off one end of the wrapping and broke a piece of bread off. Aldous offered Jasper the piece. Jasper took the offered bread and immediately shoved as much as he could into his mouth. He chewed quickly to get the rest into his mouth. Aldous broke off another piece of bread before wrapping the rest up and putting it back in the bag.

Jasper finished chewing on the piece of bread he had and swallowed it. Then he looked longingly at the piece in Aldous's hand. Aldous offered the piece of bread to Jasper. Jasper took the piece and it disappeared as fast as the first piece.

"You eat as fast as the bird in the story that the king was feeding," Aldous said.

"What story?" Jasper asked.

"You have never heard The King and the little bird?" Aldous asked. Jasper shook his head. "Then I guess I will have to tell it to you."

"Okay," Jasper said.

"Once upon a time in a far off kingdom," Aldous started,

*"There lived King Mallory. King Mallory was a very happy king, who wanted for nothing. He had every possession he wanted, he had a family, and he had servants to wait on every physical need he had. One day his wife, Queen Vanessa, got sick. King Mallory sent servants to find the best doctors. The doctors came and each looked in on Queen Vanessa. Each one came to the same conclusion. She was dying of something they could not cure. King Mallory sent them all away and then sent word for any kind of healer to come and see what they could do for Queen Vanessa. Many came, but none could do anything for Queen Vanessa. Nothing anyone could do did anything to help Queen Vanessa. King Mallory tried everything, but Queen Vanessa only got sicker and sicker. Finally King Mallory sent everyone away, even the servants that tended to her. Only one guard would not go, no matter what King Mallory threatened.*

*On the fifth day Queen Vanessa asked King Mallory to open a window, as she felt stifled. King Mallory got up and went to the window. He opened it all the way. King Mallory was just about to turn and go back to where he was sitting when he saw a bird sitting on a branch near the window. The bird was completely brown and very thin. King Mallory went to the tray that had what remained of the meal that was brought for Queen Vanessa and picked up the piece of bread that sat on it. He took it to the window and held a small piece of it out to the bird. The bird saw it and sang a happy note before hopping on to King Mallory's hand to get at the bread. King Mallory brought his hand inside without the bird noticing. The bird* was too intent on gobbling up the piece of bread. King Mallory got the bird to sit on a plate beside Queen Vanessa's bed. Queen Vanessa looked at the bird and smiled. King Mallory found a small dish to put water in and set it beside the bird. When the bird was done with that piece of bread he dipped his beak in the water. Then he looked around as if asking for more food. King Mallory slowly fed the bird a little bit at a time. The bird went through the bread so fast that King Mallory had the guard step outside and call for more from the kitchen. The bread was brought and King Mallory fed the bird half of the loaf before the bird was not interested in any more. Instead the bird went to sleep. Queen Vanessa was very pleased with the bird and hoped that it would stay, but King Mallory would not close the window in case the bird woke up and wanted to leave.

The bird was still sleeping on the plate when King Mallory, Queen Vanessa and the guard woke up the next morning. King Mallory fed the bird and made sure that the water dish was full all that day. After lunch Queen Vanessa felt strong enough to sit up. While she was sitting up she reached out and petted the bird. She found that her fingers came away muddy. So Queen Vanessa had the guard ask the servants to bring a birdbath. The servants brought it and set it up next to the table that the bird was resting on. The bird went to the bath almost immediately after the servants left the room. It splashed around until the mud started washing off. The bird turned out to be a light blue in colour. King Mallory and Queen Vanessa had never seen or heard of a bird by that colour. The guard had heard stories about birds like that and knew them to be good fortune. Queen Vanessa was so happy about the bird and the fortune it brought that she wanted King Mallory to close the window so that they could keep it. Though it displeased his wife King Mallory would not allow the window to be closed. He felt that the bird was a free creature of the earth and as such should have the right to be free if it chose. If the bird stayed then Queen Vanessa could treat it as a pet. So Queen Vanessa and King Mallory took very good care of the bird that King Mallory had brought in the window. Queen Vanessa's condition seemed to be getting better while the bird was there and King Mallory was happy.

One day Queen Vanessa took a turn for the worst and found that she could not even lift her own head. King Mallory found that the bird had flown *away when Queen Vanessa wanted him to bring it where she could see it. Queen Vanessa blamed her down turn on the bird leaving and got angry with King Mallory for letting the bird go. But King Mallory only said that the bird was a free creature of the earth and was not meant to be caged. When Queen Vanessa got angrier with him King Mallory told her that he had been given the rule over men not animals. Queen Vanessa did not get any better as time went by and King Mallory got worried again. He was scared that his wife would die soon.*

*The day Queen Vanessa slipped in to a deep sleep King Mallory got up to close the window because he thought she looked like she might be cold. Before he could close it he saw the bird sitting on the same branch it had been when he found it the first time. This time the bird was its normal light blue colour and had a branch with leaves in its beak. King Mallory reached out and the bird placed the branch it his hand. Suddenly King Mallory knew that it would cure his wife and how to make the tea to use as the cure. The bird flew away. King Mallory brought his hand in with the branch. Immediately he called for everything he needed for the tea. Using all of the leaves King Mallory made the tea and then slowly fed it to his wife. And then he waited by her side. On the second day Queen Vanessa woke up from her slumber. She had been healed from her illness by the tea.*

*King Mallory never saw the light blue bird ever again, but they say that a light blue bird appeared at his funeral. It sang a sad song in a tree before disappearing again.*

Jasper looked up at Aldous.

"Is that story really true?" Jasper asked.

"I do not know," Aldous answered, "I have only heard it once and that was when I was a boy."

"It is a really good story," Jasper said.

"Thank you," Aldous replied.

"I have to get back now," Jasper said as he stood up.

"Perhaps we will see each other again," Aldous said.

"I hope so," Jasper said. Then he disappeared into the shadows that he came out of. Aldous sat there for several more minutes before he heard footfalls of at least two people. He looked and saw two guards coming down the street. Aldous slipped into his shelter and out of sight. He made sure he took his bag with him. The guards passed by the alley a few minutes later. They looked in the alley, but they did not see Aldous. Aldous could hear them continue along the street and turn on to the next one before the footfalls died away. Jasper did not come back, but Aldous felt that the boy's leaving was due to the guards going passed.

Aldous made himself comfortable and stayed out of sight so that he could watch what happened along this street. It was not much. A few women and children went out and did a few things before disappearing back inside minutes before a two-guard patrol went by. At supper time, men came back to their homes and went inside. There was no light from any of the houses shining into the street when it got dark. Aldous ate the rest of the loaf of bread by the little bit of moonlight that trickled down to the alley. He made himself comfortable and went to sleep even with the guards still coming past at regular intervals.

In the morning, Aldous waited until after the first set of patrol men went passed before slipping out of his hiding place and going back to the market. He found the meat pie vender and bought a pie. He ate it on his way to the cider vender across the market place. The cider vender welcomed him with a smile. Today Aldous bought a skin of cider. The cider vender wished Aldous good luck as he took the money. Aldous nodded. He turned and followed a road that led out of the market place and towards the street he wanted to be on. One road later he was on the correct road. Halfway down he reached the bakery from the day before. Aldous stepped inside. There were several customers waiting. Aldous stood in line and waited for his turn to come. While he was waiting several more customers came in. No one looked at him twice despite the fact that he did not look like he should have enough money for the bread sold here as most of the other customers were the level below nobility and servants of nobility.

When Aldous got to the head of the line, Odoric smiled at him, but did not say anything that did not have to do with Aldous coming to buy two loaves of bread. Once he had paid for the loaves of bread and had been given the wrapped bundle, Aldous left the bakery. He headed back to his hiding spot in the alley where he had left his bag. The bag was still where he left it and no guards had searched the alley, but Aldous did have to be careful to avoid the patrol that was coming through as he got back to the street. He hid and waited for them to pass before he went to his alley. Once in the alley, Aldous put the loaves of bread in the bag. Again he kept watch over the street to see what happened and when.

In the middle of the day, Aldous saw two children coming through the collapsed building into the alley. Even though they were still in the shadows Aldous recognized Jasper as one of the boys. The boys finished climbing through and they looked around.

"He is not here," the boy Aldous did not recognize said.

"I told you he might not be," Jasper replied.

"Good afternoon," Aldous greeted the boys as he came out of his hiding spot. Both boys turned to face him. The second boy was the same age and skinniness as Jasper, but had shorter hair.

"This is Leander," Jasper told Aldous.

"Nice to meet you," Aldous said to Leander.

"Hello," Leander said.

"I told Leander about the story you told me yesterday," Jasper said, "And we were wondering if you would tell us a story today."

"I could do that," Aldous said as he sat down on the rock from the day before. Jasper and Leander also found rocks to sit on.

"Which would you like to hear?" Aldous asked the boys, "The unicorn and the noble's son or two elves and one shoe." The boys looked at each other and discussed the choice in whispers for a few seconds. Then they both turned back to Aldous.

"Two elves and one shoe," Jasper said.

"Once upon a time," Aldous started,

*"There lived an elf. His name was Hollis and he lived in an old shoe. He found the shoe one day when he was wandering the field looking for food. It looked like someone had lost the shoe and left it behind as there was grass growing close enough that it had not been a recent loss. He moved right in and was quite comfortable. In the summer he gathered food and played with the mice that lived in the field. In the winter he had a blanket he had woven for himself and he slept in the toes area. He ate what he had gathered during the summer. A couple times one of the mice from the field needed some place to stay and the elf willing shared the shoe because when mice stayed they warmed the shoe right up and the elf was comfortable."*

Aldous stopped the story because he could hear footfalls on the street that said that guards were approaching, which was strange since the patrol had been passed not that long ago. Aldous grabbed the boys' hands and pulled them into the hiding space. They made it out of sight just as the guards came into view. The guards did not continue down the street this time. They stopped in front of a house that was a little down and across the street from the alleyway. One guard knocked on the door. A moment later the door opened and a woman stood there. She looked scared and there was a little boy hiding behind her skirt. The guards asked for someone. The woman shook her head as she answered. The guards pushed passed her and into the house. The woman stepped outside with her son, who she clutched to her. The guards came out several minutes later dragging a man that had been knocked out.

"Poor Magdalen," Jasper whispered, "With her husband gone, she and Robin will starve." The guards dragged the man away as the woman broke down in tears before taking her son back inside. Once they could not hear the guards anymore Aldous and the boys climbed out of the hiding spot. Aldous sat back down on the rock and the boys sat down where they had been.

"Finish the story," Leander said, "Where does the other elf come into things?"

"Well," Aldous said,

"*Everything was going well for the elf living in the shoe. One winter's day the elf woke up to a scratching noise from outside the shoe. The elf got up and looked out. Three mice were outside. They were carrying another elf. This elf was asleep and looked to be half frozen.*

*'We found this elf in the snow,' one of the mice said, 'He seemed to be in need of help so we decided to bring him to you.'*

*'I will see what I can do,' the elf said. One of the mice brought the elf in to the shoe before all three mice left. The first elf wrapped the second elf in the blanket and placed him in the small space in the toe of the shoe that was warmest. The second elf started to look warmer, but he was still asleep.*

*The second elf continued to sleep. He slept for a week curled up in the toe of the shoe. The first elf was very thankful that he had two blankets, though he wished he could curl up in the toe of the shoe where it was warmest. As the weather got colder over the course of that week the first elf was grumbling about the second elf's presence because he rarely got as cold as he was. In fact by the end of the week the first elf was severely annoyed at the second elf being in his house. Even though the second elf did not eat any food or wake up and talk to the first elf, the first elf was not happy that he was there.*

*One day the mice arrived back at the shoe. The first elf went out to talk to them.*

*'How is the elf that we found half frozen?' one of the mice asked.*

*'He still has not woken up yet,' the elf answered, 'But he is breathing and he is warm.'*

*'We are here to invite you to our hole for supper this evening,' the mouse said.*

*'That sounds wonderful,' the elf said. He remembered dining with the mice before and it was always a good time.*

*'It the other elf wakes up before you have to come,' the mouse said, 'He is welcome as well.'*

'If he is awake I will tell him,' the first elf promised. The mice went away and the elf went back inside the shoe. He looked at the second elf, but the second elf had not stirred. The first elf went about the rest of his day doing the things he needed to get done for the day.

The time came for him to head out for the mouse hole. He thought of just leaving, but decided that he should keep his promise. So he went over and checked on the second elf. The second elf was still asleep. The first elf shook his shoulder, but it did not disturb the second elf. He tickled his toes, but it did not disturb the second elf. He shouted in his ear, but it did not disturb the second elf. The first elf decided that nothing would wake the second elf and off he went to the mice hole.

When he arrived he was welcomed in. The mice asked about the second elf. The first elf told him that he had tried to wake him up to no avail. The mice were sorry that the second elf would miss the party, but they were going to continue as planned.

Dinner was just as good as the elf remembered previous dinners being. He ate, he drank, and he was merry. And the mice did the same. Well, midnight came and the elf decided that he should get home. The mice told him to be careful out there. The elf said he would and he stepped outside. Because of the noise of the party no one had heard the storm blow in. Now the elf was out in a blizzard. It was so bad that even at ground level the wind was just about strong enough to carry the poor little elf away. The elf struggled through the snow and the wind anyway. But it was tiring and the party had already left the elf tired. The elf felt more than half frozen when he thought he could make out the shoe that was his home in the distance. But he was tired and he found himself falling regularly. It took more energy to pick himself up each time and his home seemed to get further and further away. The elf was not sure when he blacked out, but he remember that just before he did he thought he was going to die.

The elf woke up. He sat up and looked around. He was lying in the toe of the shoe that he lived in. The shoe had been cleaned and he had been wrapped in both blankets. But the other elf was nowhere in sight. The elf crawled out of the toes and looked outside. It was still storming.

When the mice came around after the storm the elf told them the story. They all sat and wondered about the elf, but no one had any answers. But *from then on the elf took in any creature that needed his help and he did it with a glad heart.*

Aldous finished the story and turned to the boys.

"That was a good story," Leander said.

"I like your stories," Jasper said.

"Thank you," Aldous said, "I enjoy telling stories so I like people that are interested in hearing them."

"We can come back again," Jasper said.

"If you are not needed to do something else," Aldous said, "I would be glad to tell you a story."

"Hopefully we will see you tomorrow," Leander said with a smile as he and Jasper got up off the rocks they had been sitting on.

"Before you go," Aldous said, "I have something for you to take home." The boys turned back to him. Aldous dug in to the hiding place and pulled out one of the two loaves he had bought from Odoric. He handed the loaf to Jasper.

"Thank you," Jasper said with a grin. Then he and Leander crawled back into the collapsed building. Aldous watched the boys go back through the collapsed building. Then he hid in time to avoid being seen by the patrol going passed. He waited until the footfalls on the stones of the road were out of hearing range before coming out of his hiding spot. Aldous checked how many coins he had in his pouch. He added up how much he had spent today, multiplied it by thirty days and kept that much. Looking at the rest of it he split it in half and put the amount he planned to keep back into the pouch. Then he used a strip of cloth to bundle the coins up that he had left out. It was not enough to truly compensate the woman for the loss of her husband, but Aldous hoped it would be enough that she would survive until Casimir decided on how to stop Garibold.

Aldous walked into the street being careful of who was around. He knocked on the door that the guards had. The woman opened the door moments later. Her tear stained face was set for whatever bad news that was to be given to her.

"I have something for you," Aldous said, holding out the cloth bundle, "It is not much, but I hope it helps." The woman looked at it a moment before taking it. A cry from inside made the woman go inside before she had a chance to open the bundle. Aldous closed the door before going back to his hiding spot in the alley. He sat there and watched the happenings on the street for a long time. When evening started to fall Aldous took out the last loaf of bread and the skin of cider. He ate and drank what he wanted before putting those away. Then he went to sleep.

The next morning Aldous woke up and looked around. Everything was exactly as it had been the day before. Aldous snuck out of the alley and avoided all guards on his way to the market place. Aldous bought a meat pie from the pie vender and a mug of cider from the cider vender. He ate and drank those while sitting on the low wall. He was watchful of guards and was able to give the mug back to the cider vender before seeing any guards. The guards did not appear to have any interest in him, but still Aldous left the market place once he saw them. He stopped at Odoric's bakery next. Odoric was busy with customers. Aldous waited in line behind everyone else. No one came in after Aldous did. Once Odoric was finished with everyone else and was just about to ask Aldous what he wanted today a man in expensive clothes came in and stepped in front of Aldous.

"I'm here to get the order for the castle," the man said waving a piece of paper. Then the man started reading off what he needed and Odoric had no choice but to start putting the order together. By the time the order had been put together and the man left most of Odoric's shelves were empty.

"That is what happens when the castle needs food," Odoric said, "And I am forced to spend the day trying to sell the little I have left before I close for the day."

"Why do you not bake extra for the days when the castle needs food?" Aldous asked.

"Because it is impossible to tell which day they will come," Odoric answered, "They came today and they might come again tomorrow, or they could wait for two days or sometimes they wait a week before coming back."

"That is not good," Aldous said.

"What did you want?" Odoric asked.

"Two loaves of bread," Aldous answered.

"That I have," Odoric said. He carefully wrapped up the last two loaves of bread and gave them to Aldous.

"Thank you," Aldous gave Odoric the money before accepting the bread.

"Be careful," Odoric said. Aldous took the bread and left Odoric's bakery. He snuck back into the alley and was in his hiding spot just in time to be out of sight when the patrol went by.

In the middle of the afternoon a woman who Aldous did not recognize came into the alley. She was dressed in rags and looked under fed. She was looking for something, or somebody.

"Jasper said that there was a nice man living here," the woman said out loud, "I was wondering if you were still here because I wanted to thank you for the bread that you sent with the boys yesterday."

Aldous came out of his hiding place.

"You are welcome," Aldous said.

"My name is Chrissy," the woman said.

"Ralston," Aldous said.

"I was wondering if you needed a place to stay," Chrissy said.

"I am fine where I am, thank you," Aldous said, "But perhaps I can come to supper."

"We do not have much, but you are certainly welcome to come," Chrissy said.

"I will be there for supper then," Aldous said.

"Okay," Chrissy said before turning. She glanced back before leaving the alleyway. Aldous went back into his hiding spot and continued to watch the street.

When it came close to supper time, Aldous took both loaves of bread and what was left of the cider skin and went to the house on the other side of the collapsed building from the alleyway. He knocked on the door and Jasper opened it.

"You came," Jasper said.

"Of course I did," Aldous said as he stepped inside. The room was bare except for some pillows on the floor. Aldous figured that it must be the sitting room. Jasper closed the door behind Aldous. There was a set of stairs to the left and a doorway in the wall across from the door Aldous just came in.

"And I brought some food," Aldous said.

"Chrissy is through here," Jasper said before leading the way through the doorway. Aldous followed. This room was the kitchen with stove and cupboards. Another doorway was to the left and Aldous could see a table with several mismatched chairs. He figured that it was the dining room. Chrissy was standing at the stove. She was stirring a pot of something that smelled like soup.

"Ralston is here," Jasper said. Chrissy turned around.

"Hello, Ralston," Chrissy smiled.

"Good evening," Aldous said, "I brought some bread and cider." He held up the items.

"Wonderful," Chrissy said. She went over and took them from Aldous. "The soup is just about ready."

"Our dining room is this way," Jasper led Aldous out of the kitchen to the doorway on the left. The table was set for nine people.

"Everyone else is upstairs," Jasper said, "Chrissy wanted us to look our best for your visit." Aldous nodded. "Will you tell us another story?"

"Perhaps after supper," Aldous answered.

"Do you have any about dragons?" Jasper asked as he sat down in one of the places at the table.

"I know one with a dragon," Aldous answered, "The Dragon and the Princess." Jasper made a thoughtful face.

"I guess that would be okay," Jasper said, "The girls might like that there is a princess in it."

"Jasper, will you go call the others?" Chrissy asked as she came in with a plate of sliced bread and a jug of cider.

"Yes," Jasper answered as Chrissy put the bread on the table.

"Pick whichever seat you want," Chrissy told Aldous before going back into the kitchen. Jasper got out of his chair and followed Chrissy into the kitchen. Aldous poured everyone a glass of cider before he sat down in the chair at the end of the table. A few minutes later all seven children came into the dining room and sat down. Aldous guessed that the ages of the children ranged from three to ten. They all looked unfed and ragged, but happy. Chrissy brought the soup into the dining room. She ladled out the soup into the bowls in front of everyone before taking the pot back into the kitchen. All the children sat and waited for Chrissy to come back. Chrissy came back into the dining room and sat down at the other end of the table. Only once she was ready to start eating did the children start eating.

The soup was a little thin, but Aldous found it still tasted good. The bread, of course, was Odoric's best and the cider was as good as the mug he had this morning. Everyone seemed to enjoy the food.

When the food was gone and the dishes had been cleared, everyone gathered in the sitting room. Aldous became the centre of attention and everyone else sat facing him. Chrissy had gone and found some mending she had to do before sitting with the children on the pillows.

"Once upon a time," Aldous started,

*"There lived a princess. She lived in the most beautiful palace, she had the most beautiful dresses and she lived a very happy life. Until one day a*

dragon attacked the kingdom. The dragon started with a village, burning down the houses and eating up the people. Well, the news of this spread quickly and everyone headed for the capital city as fast as they could. The king was a kind man and opened the doors to the caverns below the palace so that the people could go someplace safe. The princess did not want to go into the caverns because it was dark in there and she did not like darkness. She was young and naïve about the dangers of dragons. Meanwhile, the dragon had come to the next village to continue terrorizing the kingdom. He burned the village to the ground, but no people came running out for him to eat. Which disappointed him greatly. The dragon burned the next three villages with the same result. This made him very angry. But he realized that the delicious people were all hiding in the capital city and when he attacked the city he would probably get more than enough humans to satisfy him. So he flew over the villages and small towns until he reached the high walls of the capital city. The guards in the high towers of the city walls gave the warning call to the rest of the city. Out of the gates rode the knights of the kingdom to defend the kingdom. The dragon saw the knights and landed in the field outside the walls. The knights attacked the dragon over and over again but none of their weapons could get through the dragon's scales. The dragon would occasionally snap at the knights with his powerful jaws or take a playful swipe with his claws.

Finally the dragon got hungry so he ate up a knight, horse and all. This, of course, made the other knights try harder to kill the dragon. And the dragon played with the knights a little longer before he got hungry again and ate another knight. The knights decided to try some strategy in their attacks. The dragon watched with amusement as they carefully planned their next attack. When they finally attacked the dragon pretended to be wounded while still downing another knight. The knights regrouped and came at the dragon again. The dragon managed to eat two knights this time before the knights retreated to regroup. With so many of their numbers gone the knights were hesitant to attack again. Some of the knights went back into the city walls and rolled out a strange contraption. The dragon was interested in seeing what this contraption did and left the knights alone while they set it up. Half an hour later they had it set up. The contraption shot a net at the dragon, which covered the dragon pinning him to the ground. Then the *knights attacked. Well, the dragon did not like that. He ripped the net and shook it off before breathing fire and roasting the knights. Then the dragon ate all the knights and crushed the contraption.*

*However, the dragon was now tired and decided to take a nap before finishing his attack on the capital city."*

Aldous stopped the story. The youngest two children had fallen asleep and the rest looked like they were barely keeping their eyes open.

"I think I will tell you the rest of the story another day," Aldous said.

"Perhaps you can come for supper tomorrow night and finish it after that," Chrissy suggested.

"That would be a good idea," Aldous said. Then Chrissy ushered the children upstairs to bed. Aldous left the house and went back to his alley. He had just gotten back to his hiding spot when he heard the approaching footfalls of the patrol. Aldous closed his eyes and went to sleep.

Aldous woke up to the sounds of the patrol going by. Once the sounds had died away, Aldous got out of his hiding spot and stretched. Leaving the alley he was very careful going down the street. He headed for the market place, being very watchful of his surroundings. In the market place there were several guards standing around the fountain in the centre. Aldous went to the pie vender.

"Good morning," the pie vender greeted Aldous.

"Good morning," Aldous replied.

"How was work yesterday?" the pie vender asked as he got a meat pie for Aldous.

"Could be better," Aldous responded as he placed the money on the counter area of the cart.

"So, about usual," the pie vender said.

"Yup," Aldous said, taking the pie.

"Try to have a good day," the pie vender said.

"You too," Aldous replied. He ate the pie as he strode purposefully across the market place to where the cider vender was.

"Good morning," the cider vender greeted Aldous.

"Good morning," Aldous replied.

"Mug or skin, today?" the cider vender asked.

"Skin," Aldous answered, "I do not have time to enjoy a mug today." The cider vender got a skin of cider for Aldous. Aldous gave the cider vender the money as he took the skin.

"Have a good day," the cider vender said.

"You too," Aldous said. Then he left the market place as if he had to get to work. He kept that pace up until he reached Odoric's bakery then he stopped and went inside. Today the line up of customers was very short when Aldous was inside. Odoric dealt with the customers in his usual speed. And finally Aldous and Odoric were the only ones in the small shop.

"Good morning," Odoric greeted Aldous.

"Good morning," Aldous replied.

"Two loaves of bread?" Odoric asked.

"Yes, please," Aldous answered.

"There is someone from the castle who can give you information on what is going on there," Odoric said as he wrapped up the two loaves of bread.

"Who?" Aldous asked.

"Faye," Odoric answered.

"She was the cook's daughter, was she not?" Aldous asked.

"She has been moved up to cleaning rooms," Odoric answered, "She comes in here on days she is sent to get something. She has been bringing me bits and pieces of information since I was forced to leave. It would not be that much trouble to get her to bring you information."

"Where would I meet her?" Aldous asked.

"The alleyway behind my shop," Odoric answered, "I would tell you when you came in to buy your bread in the morning when she is in town."

"That would work," Aldous said.

"I will let her know the next time that I see her," Odoric said.

"That would be good," Aldous said. Aldous gave Odoric the money for the bread and Odoric gave Aldous the bread.

"Good day," Aldous said.

"Good day," Odoric said. Aldous left Odoric's bakery and headed back to his hiding spot in the alley. He had to stay out of sight between two buildings while the patrol went passed before he could get to the alley and his hiding spot. Once in the alley Aldous tucked the loaves of bread and the skin of cider into his sack before getting out of his hiding spot.

Aldous checked the street carefully before going back out, but this time he went in the opposite direction from his usual excursions. He went several streets down and as he went the houses showed less wear and the people that were out were dressed a lot better. A few looked down their noses at him, though most did not even notice him. Aldous did not blame people for looking down on him. He looked like a dirty, old beggar. But he walked with enough purpose that no one was going to call the guard on him.

Aldous walked passed these houses to ones of more expensive taste, where many of the nobles lived. It was not much farther that he reached the house of Lord Scatchern. The man had been one of the few people that Aldous would have called his friend. Aldous doubted that Lord Scatchern would have been allowed to maintain his position in court, but Lord Scatchern would still be present in court just the same. As much as Aldous would have liked to ring the bell and talk to his friend, Aldous instead went to the back of the house. At the back of the house was a lookout that Lord Scatchern's father had built so that he could watch what his neighbours were doing. He had done it so that it did not look like a lookout and no one on the ground could tell who was up there.

Aldous climbed over the fence and went up the ladder that led up to the lookout. From there Aldous could see all of Lord Scatchern's neighbours and the street in front of the house. Aldous noticed that everyone kept busy and no one on the street stopped to talk. What really surprised Aldous was that there were regular patrols along this street just as there were along the poor street. And guards were making demands of anyone that did not appear to be doing anything. Aldous even watched as one unlucky lad did not give the right answer and was dragged away by the guards.

It was getting to be afternoon when Aldous heard someone coming up the ladder. Aldous turned to see the head of a boy come into view. Aldous guessed the boy to be Aurick, Lord Scatchern's grandson. The boy looked at Aldous as if he was not sure whether he wanted to go the way up, but then Aurick finished coming up the ladder. He had a smile on his face.

"Aldous," Aurick said coming towards Aldous with his arms out to get a hug. Aldous hugged him. When Aldous had left the boy had only been four, now he looked half grown.

"Hello, Aurick," Aldous said once the boy let go.

"What are you doing here?" Aurick asked, "Grandfather said that you were captured in battle."

"I was," Aldous said, "By King Casimir. But he let me come back here so that I could help him."

"He wants to stop Advisor Jarlath from taking over Lithimin," Aurick said.

"That is right," Aldous said.

"Grandfather is angry that Prince Garibold is letting Advisor Jarlath run the kingdom," Aurick said, "Grandfather says that Advisor Jarlath is running the kingdom into the ground, but Mother said that Advisor Jarlath is only ruining the reputation of the kingdom. Who is right?"

"They both are," Aldous answered, "Jarlath is destroying the integrity of the kingdom, which is why he is running it into the ground, but by destroying the integrity he is also ruining the reputation built by the royal line."

"That makes sense," Aurick said, "But why are you here and not in the castle trying to stop them?"

"You have seen the army," Aldous said.

"Father was forced to join," Aurick said with a nod.

"If I were to go to the castle and declare myself, what do you think would happen to me?" Aldous asked.

"Advisor Jarlath would not like it and he would have you locked up or worse," Aurick answered.

"So, there is another plan," Aldous said, "I am here to gather information so that the other plan will work."

"Grandfather would like to know the other plan," Aurick said, "He is depressed at what has been happening to the kingdom."

"I know," Aldous said, "But it is better if he does not know. And I hope you will not tell anyone about seeing me or me being in the kingdom."

"You are still in prison in Lithimin," Aurick said.

"Yes," Aldous said.

"Is there anything I can do to help with your plan?" Aurick asked.

"Yes," Aldous answered, "Keep listening to your grandfather and if we see each other up here you can tell me what is going on in court."

"I can do that," Aurick said, "Grandfather wants me to know what is going on in court and the rest of the kingdom because he says that if something does not happen soon I will be taking over instead of Father. But if I can help with the plan then maybe Father will come back and everything will be all right."

"Everything will be all right," Aldous said, "It just might take a month."

"That is okay," Aurick said, "So, what are you doing up here?"

"Watching people," Aldous answered, "Seeing how people react to the guards, how the guards react to the people, and how things have changed in the last five years."

"Do you mind if I watch with you?" Aurick asked, "Grandfather will not be home from court for another hour at least."

"I do not mind if you watch with me," Aldous answered. The two of them stood at the railing and watched the people.

An hour later, they saw Lord Scatchern come home. Aurick went down the ladder and into the house. Aldous watched his old friend. Like himself, Lord Scatchern looked older, but Lord Scatchern also looked far more worn. Knowing that he could not erase any of the lines off his friend's face Aldous made a silent promise that it would all be over in a month. Lord Scatchern went inside the house. Aldous stayed up there for another hour.

When Aldous finally climbed down he carefully avoided the guards that were out in what seemed to be greater numbers and headed back to the alley and his hiding spot. Once there Aldous took out the bread and the cider skin. He took them and knocked on Chrissy's door. Jasper opened the door before Aldous was even finished knocking.

"Hello," Jasper said as Aldous stepped inside.

"Good evening," Aldous replied. All the children were in the sitting room waiting. Jasper closed the door. Aldous took the bread and cider into the kitchen, where Chrissy accepted them where she was making another pot of soup. Aldous went back out to the sitting room.

"So, what did you do all day?" Aldous asked.

"Uria across the street holds classes," Jasper answered, "She is trying to teach us to read and deal with numbers."

"Those are very good skills to have," Aldous said.

"But the only book she has is boring," Jasper said, "It is all about some saint's beliefs."

"Saint Ada," the oldest girl said, "The saint of washmaids, who has to be the most boring saint there is. There are like twelve blessings for white shirts alone, depending on what type of material they are made out of."

"It is really boring," Leander said.

"But at least you are learning to read," Aldous said.

"That is what Chrissy keeps saying," the oldest girl said, "But it would be better if we had something better to read."

"Time for supper," Chrissy called from the kitchen. All the children got up and ran towards the dining room. Aldous followed at a much slower pace. Everyone else was seated and waiting when he got to the dining room. Aldous sat down in the only chair left, which was at the head of the table. And everyone started to eat.

After supper was finished and everything was cleaned up everyone gathered in the sitting room.

"Now, where was I?" Aldous asked.

"The dragon had eaten all the knights and was taking a nap before attacking the rest of the city," Jasper answered.

"Where does the princess come in?" one of the girls asked.

"You will have to listen to find out," Aldous answered,

*"When the dragon had woken up he looked around as he stretched. Everything looked the same as when he went to sleep. He could still smell that there were humans in the city. The dragon breathed fire at the gates, but the gates did not even look singed. The dragon did not bother with a second attempt. He just flew over the walls. He breathed fire at a few buildings, but no people came out. The dragon left the rest of the houses alone and headed straight to the palace. He followed the scent of human to one of the towers. Inside the tower was the princess's room, where the princess and her guard were. The guard had tried to get her to go to the caverns or someplace farther inside the palace, but the princess refused and the guard had given up.*

*The dragon got close enough that he could see in the window. He saw the guard and the princess. Well, the dragon thought the guard looked tasty, but princesses were not very good eating. There was very little meat on the bones. You have to eat a whole lot of princesses to make a meal out of them and the dragon only saw one princess. However, the dragon did like to collect princesses. He had a cage back at his cave that he kept them in. They were very useful as bait too. So the dragon reached in the tower window. He pulled out the princess and her guard. The guard he ate in one gulp. The dragon burped before flying off with the princess. He took her back to his cave and put her in the cage that hung from the ceiling of his cave. Then the dragon lay down on the piles of gold and fell asleep.*

*The princess was scared and hanging in the cage above the sleeping dragon made her realize how foolish she had been. Now if she could only figure out some way to get out. The princess looked around the cave. There was a lot of gold, jewels, and other treasure. There was a stack of swords, armour and shields from knights that had tried to attack the dragon. None of it was within her reach. In fact she could only barely get the cage to swing on the chain and it squealed when it moved. When the chain squealed the dragon's ears moved as if the dragon would wake up if the princess got close to escaping."*

Aldous stopped because the youngest two were asleep and the rest looked on their way there.

"Perhaps I can come back and finish it tomorrow evening," Aldous said.

"Looks like it," Chrissy said.

"But I wanna hear the rest," Jasper said through a yawn.

"You will," Chrissy said, "But tomorrow." She ushered the children upstairs. Aldous left the house and went back to the alley. He went into his hiding spot and went to sleep.


Aldous woke up to the sound of a cart going along the street. Aldous looked out his hiding spot. It was just a vender cart that was headed for the market place. Aldous looked up at what he could see of the sky. It was the usual time he woke up. The vender was going to be late to set up. Aldous crawled out of his hiding spot and stretched. There was an air of oppression over the city. Aldous could feel it. He was extra careful as he left the alley and wandered towards the market place. As he got closer Aldous found more and more guards around. It was getting closer when Aldous saw Jasper in an alleyway. Aldous went in to the alleyway. Jasper and Leander were seated in crates.

"What is going on?" Aldous's voice was hushed.

"Prince Garibold is holding court in the market place," Jasper answered. Jasper pointed to the opening at the other end of the alleyway. There were two guards near the entrance to the alleyway. Aldous went passed Jasper and Leander and crept to the other end of the alleyway. From there Aldous could see the throne set up for Garibold and the men that were being tried. Garibold was sitting on the throne. He still looked like a boy to Aldous. He also looked like he had no interest in being there. The man standing just behind Garibold's throne was the nobleman, Jarlath. Jarlath regularly leaned in to whisper something in Garibold's ear. It was like watching a puppet show.

Men were brought forward and their crime was announced. They were given the choice between joining the army and going to prison. All the men picked prison. And the amount of time they were to serve was announced and the next man was brought forward. Aldous did not hear any terms that were less than thirty years and most of the crimes were things like loitering. Aldous shook his head as he withdrew in to the alleyway. He went back to where Jasper and Leander were.

"Prince Garibold is not a good ruler," Jasper said.

"No, he is not," Aldous replied, "But he is the one that is here."

"Maybe another country will attack us and kill him and then we can be ruled by the leader of that country," Leander said.

"With the size of the army Prince Garibold has gathered?" Aldous said, "I do not think that is possible."

"I do not want to end up in one of Prince Garibold's courts," Jasper said.

"Then you need to stay out of trouble," Aldous said. Aldous started out of the alleyway.

"Where are you going?" Jasper asked.

"To find breakfast," Aldous answered.

"Can we come?" Jasper asked. His eyes lit up at the word breakfast.

"Sure," Aldous answered, "But we have to be careful and stay out of sight of the guards."

"That is easy," Jasper said, "Leander and I do that all the time." Jasper and Leander stood up and went with Aldous. They even showed Aldous some short cuts that kept them out of sight of the guards. Finally they reached Odoric's bakery. Even from the outside Aldous could tell that there were no customers inside, but it was open. Aldous opened the door and the three of them stepped inside. The boys looked at all the baked goods and they were just about drooling. Odoric laughed to see their faces.

"Been a very long time since I have had children in my bakery," Odoric said.

"I offered to buy them breakfast," Aldous said, "Since the market place is closed for the day."

"Bad tidings on that," Odoric said shaking his head, then he turned to the boys, "You each can pick something. What do you want?"

"That one, sir," Leander pointed to something. Odoric got one and gave it to the boy.

"Here you go," Odoric said. Leander took it. Jasper looked at everything and could not seem to decide until he finally picked something.

"That one," Jasper said, pointing at what he wanted. Odoric got one for him and handed it to him.

"Here you go," Odoric said.

"Two loaves of bread and a pastry," Aldous said.

"Coming right up," Odoric said. He got a pastry and handed it to Aldous before starting to wrap up the loaves of bread. Aldous started to eat the pastry. When they boys saw Aldous eating, they ate up their food as well. They were finished eating at the same time Odoric had finished wrapping up the bread. Odoric gave Aldous the loaves of bread and Aldous paid for everything.

"There was a young woman looking for you this morning," Odoric told Aldous before Aldous could turn to go, "She said she would be back later this morning in case you stop by."

"Thank you," Aldous said, "I will see if I can find her in a few minutes."

"If she comes back before then I will tell her," Odoric said. Aldous turned and the boys followed him as he left the bakery.

"Who is the woman?" Jasper asked.

"A friend," Aldous answered, "Just like you are my friends."

"Oh," Jasper said.

"Now let us get back before trouble finds us," Aldous said. They headed down the street and took the first alleyway they could because they could see guards.

"What is the bread for?" Leander asked.

"Tonight's supper," Aldous answered, "The same as the loaves of bread I have bought for the last few days."

"They are always good," Jasper said. They went across a street to another alleyway.

They finally reached the right street and they had to wait for the patrol to go passed. Then Jasper and Leander went to the house with the repeated promise that Aldous would be there for supper. Aldous went to the alley. He put the bread in his sack in his hiding spot before leaving the alley again. Aldous went back to the bakery, but this time he went in to the alleyway at the back of the bakery instead of the front door.

There was no one waiting for him when Aldous arrived. Aldous found a crate in a dark part of the alleyway and sat down on it. Half an hour went by before the back door to Odoric's bakery opened. Faye stepped out of the bakery and into the alleyway. Aldous remembered Faye as a girl. But she had grown into a young woman. Aldous could see some of the long black hair that came out of her head wrap and he was pretty sure that she wrapped her chest tightly to avoid unwelcome notice. But even the dirty face held the type of beauty that nothing could hide. Faye looked around, but she did not see him. She wrapped her arms around her and leaned against the wall. It was not cold so Aldous figured that she was scared.

"Hello, Faye," Aldous said as he stood up and stepped in to the light. Faye jumped at the sound of his voice but relaxed when she saw him. She smiled at him.

"I did not believe Odoric when he said that you had come back," Faye said, "But you have."

"I have," Aldous said, "I was pardoned so that I could help King Casimir take down Garibold."

"Prince Garibold is not the problem," Faye said, "He does not want to be king. He wants his pleasures and to leave the rest alone."

"I know that Jarlath is the problem," Aldous said, "I saw the spectacle they were putting on in the market place today; a puppet king putting on a show to terrify the peasants. The people are already terrified to live, but they do not know what else to do. It saddens me not to see children playing in the street anymore."

"Then you will help King Casimir take down Prince Garibold and Jarlath?" Faye asked.

"Yes, that is why I am here," Aldous answered, "I am here to gather information so that King Casimir can breach the defences of the kingdom and take out my son in his foolishness."

"What information do you need?" Faye asked, "I will keep my ears open."

"Everything," Aldous answered, "From schedules to plans that Jarlath is making. Get what you can, but do not worry about anything you cannot get. And do not get into trouble to get information."

"I will try not to get into trouble," Faye said.

"If you do, I will not be able to get the information I need," Aldous said. Faye nodded.

"I will do what I can," Faye said.

"Thank you," Aldous said.

"I just want Prince Garibold's reign to be over," Faye said.

"From what I have seen, so do I," Aldous said. Faye nodded and went back into the bakery. Aldous stayed where he was until the door was closed. Then he headed off.

Aldous went back the way he had the day before. Up passed the merchant class houses to the houses owned by nobles and finally he arrived at Lord Scatchern's house. He went around to the back and up the ladder to the look out. Aldous positioned himself in the right place to watch all the comings and goings.

About mid afternoon someone came up the ladder. Aldous turned to look and saw Aurick's head appear at the top of the ladder. Aurick came the rest of the way up and sat down next to Aldous.

"Grandfather is home today," Aurick said, "Because Prince Garibold is holding trials in the market place, which Grandfather calls a disgusting display of power."

"I saw some of the trials," Aldous said.

"What was it like?" Aurick asked.

"Like watching innocent people being condemned," Aldous answered.

"Grandfather says that Advisor Jarlath is getting impatient with Prince Garibold," Aurick said, "Because despite everything they had done to the kingdom Prince Garibold will not break decorum and attack Lithimin. Advisor Jarlath wants King Casimir crushed under his feet and Prince Garibold will not let the army attack until the diplomats finish the peace negotiations, or until the peace negotiations collapse. So, Grandfather thinks that Advisor Jarlath will do something to try and make the peace negotiations collapse."

"King Casimir will do everything in his power to make sure that the peace negotiations do not collapse," Aldous said, "His kingdom is a stake and he will not give it up without a fight."

"If our army was not as big or as strong he could attack and not have to go through all of this," Aurick said.

"That is right," Aldous said, "But I would still be locked in his prison if it was that easy for him."

Aurick was quiet and they sat without talking as they watched the people below them.

"Is there anything else that I can do?" Aurick asked.

"I need a book of stories," Aldous said, "For some children that I have met. They are learning to read and are bored of the book that they have to use to learn to read. I was hoping I could find something else that they could read."

"Grandfather has the book of stories that you loaned him before you left," Aurick said, "It ended up among my school books. I have memorized the stories and if I forget Grandfather is always willing to tell them to me. I could get that book for you."

"That would be wonderful," Aldous said. Aurick got up and went down the ladder. He came back up a few moments later. He had the book in his hand. He gave it to Aldous. Aldous took it and flipped through it. It was the book of fables that Lord Scatchern always loved to tell. Aldous had never really liked the stories in this volume; he had always liked the stories from the other volume. But Jasper and the rest would probably like this volume, as the stories were just right for children.

"Thank you," Aldous said.

"Grandfather loves telling me those," Aurick said, "He says that he will never get tired of telling me those, even when I am an adult and have children of my own."

"Your grandfather is a very good story teller," Aldous said.

"But never as good as you are," Aurick said, "I miss hearing you tell stories, because every time you told me stories they always seemed to come to life in my head, even the ones I did not like."

"Perhaps you can hear me tell stories again some time," Aldous said.

"Maybe when Advisor Jarlath and Prince Garibold are out of power," Aurick said.

"That would be a good time," Aldous said. Aldous flipped through the book some more. He saw a page with something scribbled on it. He went back and found the page. On it in Lord Scatchern's handwriting was a poem.

*Aldous did not know what to do,*
*So he decided to tell a story or two,*
*He looked around for a child,*
*But could not find one for a mile,*
*So Aldous was forced to think of something else to do.*

Aldous laughed when he finished reading the poem.

"What is it?" Aurick asked.

"The poem that your grandfather wrote in here," Aldous answered.

"I have read it," Aurick said, "But I never found it to be funny."

"The humour has a lot to do with how long your grandfather and I have known each other," Aldous said. Aurick nodded.

"Mother was looking for me when I went and got the book," Aurick said, "So I have to get back to the house."

"I hope we will see each other soon," Aldous said.

"Me too," Aurick said, then he went down the ladder. Aldous put the book in his pocket before going back to watching the people.

When the afternoon was starting to disappear Aldous went down the ladder and walked through the streets back to the alley where his hiding spot was. Reaching the alley he dug out the two loaves of bread out of his bag before going to Chrissy's house. Jasper had the door open before Aldous could knock.

"Chrissy is not quite finished the soup," Jasper told Aldous once Aldous had stepped inside and the door had been closed.

"Okay," Aldous said. Most of the children were gathering in the sitting room again. Aldous took the bread to the kitchen and gave it to Chrissy before going back into the sitting room.

"What did you spend the day doing?" Aldous asked.

"We were not allowed out," the oldest girl answered, "So we sat here playing string games." She held up a piece of string with the ends tied together to form a circle.

"What kind of string games?" Aldous asked.

"The usual kind," the girl answered, "Have you not played games with string?"

"No, I have not," Aldous replied, "Will do you not show me one?"

"Okay," the girl said. She and another girl showed Aldous the string game and explained to him what they were doing.

"What did you do today?" Jasper asked once the demonstration was over.

"I found a book for you," Aldous answered as he pulled the volume out of his pocket. The children stared at the book.

"For us?" Jasper asked in wonder, "But books are expensive. Uria only has one because her mother left it to her."

"It is for all of you to learn to read on and to practice that skill," Aldous answered, "Because it is an important skill to learn and if you do not like what you are forced to read you will not do it."

"What is it a book of?" Leander asked as the oldest girl took the book. She handled the volume as if it was as delicate as a flower and might turn to dust any second.

"Fables," Aldous answered, "Stories like the ones I have been telling you."

"Wow," Jasper said, then his face turned serious, "Does that mean you will not finish the Dragon and the Princess?"

"I will finish the Dragon and the Princess," Aldous answered, "the book is for your enjoyment at other times."

"This is great," the oldest girl said as she opened it, "It even has pictures in it." The rest of the children crowded around her, but they were all careful not to touch the book.

"Supper is ready," Chrissy called from the kitchen. The children got up and hurried towards the dining room, except the oldest girl. She carefully placed the book on the only shelf in the room before going to the dining room. Aldous followed her. He sat down in the chair at the head of the table, because it seemed to be reserved for him. Everyone waited until Aldous and the girl were seated to start eating.

After supper was over and everything had been cleaned up everyone gathered in the sitting room with Aldous as the centre of attention.

"How is the princess going to get away from the dragon?" Jasper asked, "The dragon has her trapped in a cage. And she cannot fight the dragon even if she had a weapon. And the knights from the kingdom all got roasted and eaten. And the dragon wants someone to try and rescue her because then he can eat them."

"Jasper, let him get on with the story," the oldest girl said. Jasper sat back and was silent.

"Those are all very good points," Aldous said, "The princess does appear to be in quite a bad situation.

*She continued to look around and figure something out, but like the first time she looked around nothing that she could use was within her reach. The princess tried the door of the cage, but it was locked. And every time she walked around the chain squeaked and the dragon's ears twitched. The princess finally sat down in despair, as far as she could tell there was no way out of this situation. She fell in to a fitful sleep and had terrible dreams. When she woke the dragon was still sleeping on the piles of gold. Something had to have woken her up. She got to her knees and looked around. Listening carefully the princess could hear something besides the dragon's snoring. Finally she realized that it was the sound of horse's hooves on the stone floor of the cave. The princess thought her rescue was on its way. Finally the princess saw a knight on a horse. The knight was intent on the dragon and did not seem to notice the princess. The knight charged the sleeping dragon. The dragon woke up at just the right moment to gobble the knight up in one gulp and then go back to sleep again. The princess once again laid down in despair.*

*This went on for a week. The princess sat in the cage, the dragon slept, except to eat knights that came along, and nothing changed.*

'Is that all you do?' the princess asked the sleeping dragon one day, 'Eat and sleep.'

'Of course not,' the dragon answered, lifting his head to look at her, 'But after five centuries that is all I enjoy doing.'

'You can talk?' the princess was surprised.

'You can,' the dragon replied, 'why should I not be able to?'

'I never thought of that,' the princess said.

'Silly human,' the dragon muttered with a puff of smoke. Then the dragon lay back down and closed his eyes. The princess got an idea.

'Do you like riddles?' the princess asked.

'Silly human,' the dragon muttered before lifting his head and looking at her. He answered her, 'I might if I was a young dragon and had not heard them all before. I have had many princesses and they all try the same things to escape. None of them ever succeed.'

'I am not trying to escape,' the princess said, 'I am just bored. You are the only one to talk to since you put me in this cage. Do you like knock, knock jokes?'

'What are knock, knock jokes?' the dragon asked. There was curiosity in those metallic eyes.

'I say knock, knock and you say who is there and I say a name and you repeat the name with a who at the end and then I tell you the punch line,' the princess explained, 'Let us try one and you can see if you like it. Knock, knock.'

'Who is there?' the dragon asked.

'Ahead,' the princess answered.

'Ahead who?' the dragon asked.

'A head is on your shoulders,' the princess answered.

'That is it?' the dragon asked.

'That was a knock, knock joke,' the princess answered, 'Would you like to try another one?'

'Sure,' the dragon replied.

'Knock, knock,' the princess said.

'Who is there?' the dragon asked.

'Ach,' the princess answered.

'Ach who?' the dragon asked.

'Bless you,' the princess answered, 'Knock, knock.'

'Who is there?'

'Abbot.'

'Abbot who?'

'Abbot you do not know who this is.'

The dragon snorted with laughter.

'Knock, Knock,' the princess said.

'Who is there?' the dragon asked.

'A herd.'

'A herd who?' '

'A herd you were home, so I came over,' the princess replied. Another snort of smoke came from where the dragon was.

'Knock, knock,' the princess said.

'Who is there?' the dragon asked still cackling with laughter.

'Allmen,' the princess answered.

'Allmen who?' the dragon asked.

'Allmen act silly,' the princess replied. The dragon was now lying on its side laughing. It was having trouble catching his breath. The princess waited until the dragon was just about got its breath back.

'Knock, knock,' the princess asked.

'Who…is…ther…re?' the dragon gasped out.

'A little boy who could not reach the bell,' the princes replied. The dragon roared with laughter at that one. In fact the dragon could not stop laughing. In trying to catch his breath the dragon breathed some fire straight at the ceiling. The fire hit the rock and dispersed in either direction. The fire melted the links of the chain that were closest to the ceiling. There was another bolt in the ceiling that the chain was hooked into that was far enough away for the fire not to reach it, so when the chain broke the cage swung wildly on the other hook and banged into the wall. All of this scared the princess but she hung on to the bars to avoid being thrown around. The dragon was too busy laughing to notice all of this. Once the cage had finished its swing the princess let go of the bars and looked around. The side that hit the wall was the side of the cage with the door and now that part of the cage was caved in. There was a hole in the bars big enough for the princess to get through. She climbed through the bars and jumped to the ground, as it was *not as far as it had been. The princess jarred her ankle but that did not stop her from running for the entrance of the cave. Once outside the cave she slowed down to a walk because her ankle hurt too much.*

*The princess walked along the road until she came upon a knight riding to her rescue. The knight offered her a ride back to her kingdom, which she accepted. But she refused to tell him how she escaped. She made it home safe and her father was very happy to see her. The kingdom celebrated at her return, even though they all were still worried because the dragon was still alive.*

*Back at the cave the dragon finally got his laughter under control. He turned to the cage to ask the princess to tell another one when he saw what had happened. Realizing that the princess was gone, the dragon lay down on a pile of gold and thought to himself. While he was thinking a knight came into the cave. The knight charged him shouted something about being the evil dragon that kidnapped the princess and on the princess's honour he would defeat the dragon. The dragon roasted the knight a little and then ate him. The dragon decided as he was chewing that he could leave the princess alone. She had been the first being in three centuries to make him laugh and knights were still coming for him to eat.*

*And both lived happily ever after."*

Aldous finished the story. None of the children were asleep this time, but they all looked ready for bed.

"That was a good story," Jasper said.

"Thank you for the story, Ralston," Chrissy said, "Now, it is time for bed, children." The children did not want to go, but they let Chrissy herd them up the stairs. Aldous left the house once they were out of sight. Then he went back to his hiding place. Aldous crawled inside and went to sleep.

Aldous opened his eyes when he heard the sound of horse's hooves on the stone of the street. He looked out at the street. There were two men on horses were in the middle of the street, where they apparently had stopped to talk. Aldous recognized one of the men as Jarlath. The other man Aldous did not recognize, but it looked to be another noble. Something inside of

Aldous wanted to run out into the street and drag Jarlath off his horse and beat him with a rock until he was dead. Even if he was killed shortly after the thought said it would still be worth it. But Aldous found himself clutching the Saint Milon's medallion that he wore instead of running out in to the street. Aldous thought of what he learned about Saint Milon and the peaceful way his followers lived. This calmed him and the thought of running out into the street passed. Aldous stayed in his hiding place until the riders moved on and the patrol had gone passed. Aldous then got up and stretched before heading to the market place.

Today the market place was set up in the usual way. Aldous's first stop was the pie vender. The pie vender gave Aldous a nod before taking his money and giving him a meat pie. Aldous took the pie and ate it on his way across the market place to the cider vender. At the cider vender, Aldous stayed and talked for a few minutes while he drank the mug of cider. When he was finished Aldous gave back the mug before going on to the next street. He went along the street until he got to Odoric's bakery. Aldous went inside. There was a line up of customers and several more came in after Aldous did. Aldous bought two loaves of bread, but he and Odoric did not say much to each other.

After that Aldous went back to the alley. Jasper came out of the shadows when Aldous arrived.

"Can you tell me another story?" Jasper asked.

"Are you not suppose to be doing something else today?" Aldous asked.

"Honora is reading the book of fables you brought us and the rest are over at Uria's," Jasper said, "But I finished everything Uria gave me to do for the week and she will not give me any more until Leander has finished the same amount of work."

"Then I suppose I can tell you the story of the unicorn and the nobleman's son," Aldous said.

"Would not the nobleman's son also be a nobleman?" Jasper asked.

"Yes," Aldous said, "But that is not what the story is called."

"Okay," Jasper sat down on the rock he had been sitting on before. Aldous sat down on the bigger rock.

"Once a upon a time," Aldous started,

*A nobleman's son went out to the forest to go hunting. This nobleman's son was named Welby and he was a very good hunter. He went out with his best friend and his father's huntsman. They went deep into the forest because Welby and his friend had heard that the deer in the heart of the forest were much bigger than those that wandered the forest's edges. They camped at night and hunted during the day. Well, on the last day of their hunt they had not found any deer that fit the description of what they were looking for. They were disappointed, but determined to do better on their final day out. That morning Welby and his friend made a bet on who could get the best deer. The huntsman warned them to be careful and not to get foolish in the hunt just because they wanted to win the bet. Welby and his friend acknowledged the huntsman, but were not really listening to him. So, off they set to get the best deer for the day. They had only gone a little ways when Welby thought he heard something in the bush behind them. Thinking that it might be the deer to win the bet Welby did not tell anyone else that he heard anything, but he went in the direction of the sound. His friend and the huntsman did not notice him. Welby followed the sound as the animal ahead of him went through the brush. It was so dense in the forest that Welby could not see the creature that he was following.*

*Finally Welby came to a clearing. The creature had gotten there ahead of him so Welby stayed in the brush and aimed an arrow at the creature. He was just about to shoot when the creature fully came into view. It was not a deer, but a pure white unicorn. Welby did not shoot instead he lowered his bow. He put the bow and arrow away. The unicorn took a drink from the pool in the clearing before going off into the brush again. Welby followed the unicorn. He had never seen such an amazing creature in his life, but he could not shoot it or do it any harm. Welby followed that unicorn for hours. He was growing tired when another clearing came in view. Welby stopped and looked. The unicorn was in the clearing settling on a bed of soft moss. It seemed to be getting ready to go to sleep. Welby was tired and not sure what to do, but decided to go into the clearing. The unicorn looked up at Welby.*

Welby felt like the unicorn could see through to his soul. Suddenly Welby felt dizzy and he collapsed into unconsciousness.

Welby found himself in a strange place. He looked around, there were dark trees and the white unicorn was standing nearby. The unicorn glowed in the darkness.

'What happened?' Welby asked. His voice sounded like it came from a great distance.

'Why did you come into the forest?' the deep voice demanded.

'I was hunting with my friend,' Welby answered.

'Hunting unicorns?' the voice asked.

'No, hunting deer,' Welby answered.

'There are plenty of deer on the edges of the forest,' the voice said. Welby thought it might have been coming from the unicorn, but he could not tell.

'I was told that there were fatter deer in the middle of the forest,' Welby replied, 'And I wanted to get one.'

'And what do you wish to do with a fatter deer than you can get at the edge of the forest?' the voice answered.

'Take it back to my father's house and use it as meat for a feast,' Welby answered, 'and use the hide for clothing.'

'I am the guardian of this forest,' the voice said, 'You have come too deep into the forest. I will give you your prize, but you must promise never to come this deep again. And you must warn people that anyone else that comes this deep will never be seen from again.'

'I promise never to come this deep into the forest again,' Welby said, 'And I will warn people that if they come this deep they will never be seen from again.'

Welby found himself back at the edge of the first clearing. His bow and arrow were in his hands. And a large deer drinking from the pool that the unicorn had drank from before. Welby brought his bow up to shoot the deer, but something made him hesitate. Maybe the deer looked too much like the unicorn or maybe he realized his mistake in coming this far into the forest. He lowered his bow.

Suddenly he heard his name being called from the distance. The deer looked up from its drink and froze. Welby recognized his friend's voice when *his name was called again. The deer ran off. Welby put his bow and arrow away and headed toward the voices. He found his friend and the huntsman not that far away. They had no luck, but realized that he was missing. He told them that he had not had any luck either. They went back to the camp. Both Welby and his friend lost the bet. The next day the three of them headed back to the nobleman's house. As they were finishing packing up camp Welby thought he saw the unicorn, but it might have been a trick of the light.*

*Welby did, however, keep both his promises. He never went that deep into the forest again and he warned people against going that deep. He claimed that the best deer were on the edges of the forest anyway."*

Aldous finished the story.

"I liked that story," Jasper said as he stood up.

"Here," Aldous held out one of the loaves of bread to Jasper, "For your supper."

"Thank you," Jasper smiled as he took the loaf of bread. Then he went through the collapsed building and headed back to Chrissy's house. Aldous put the other loaf of bread in his sack before heading to the lookout behind Lord Scatchern's house.

Aldous spent the rest of the month telling stories to Jasper and the other children, talking about the affairs of the kingdom with Aurick, getting information and giving comfort to Faye, and talking with Odoric when he went to buy bread from him every morning. Nothing changed with Garibold and Jarlath and their ruling of the kingdom. And as far as anyone else could hear, nothing had changed between Proster and Lithimin.

# ALDEN FINDS KING ALDOUS AND KING CASIMIR NEEDS THE INFORMATION THAT WAS GATHERED

Aldous woke up. Not hearing anything or seeing anything on the street he got out of his hiding space and stretched. Somehow he felt like there was more hope in the air this morning. Aldous snuck out of the alleyway and made his way to the market place. Everything looked like it usually did. The guards and the people were acting as they usually did. So Aldous assumed that the feelings of hope were from him.

Aldous exchanged greetings with the pie vender as he bought a meat pie. He then went over to the cider vender, with whom he talked for a minute. Then Aldous sat down on the low wall to have his breakfast. He had just finished and was returning the mug to the cider vender when he saw two guards coming across the market place towards him. They looked like the same two guards that he had gotten into trouble with his first day in the market place. Aldous walked away as if he had not seen the guards, but he walked in his purposeful stride that was fast enough that he was around the corner to the next street before the guards had gotten across the market place. But they continued to follow him down this street. Aldous continued to the street after and, half way down, he ducked into an alley. The guards must have seen him go in to the alley because Aldous could hear them break into a run. Aldous found a dark corner behind a crate where he could hide. The guards entered the alley and stopped. They could not see him or where he went. The guards moved into the alley at a slower and much more cautious pace. They were about to reach the crate where Aldous was hiding when a shadow fell over the entrance to the alley. Aldous looked and saw a man dressed in a dark cloak standing there. The guards turned around to see what happened to the light. The person in the cloak looked bent over and had a walking stick. The guards drew their swords.

"Who are you?" one of the guards demanded as the person in the cloak started towards them. The person did not answer, just kept moving forward.

"Halt!" the other guard cried. The person straightened up as they walked forward making them taller than both guards. The guards got ready to fight. When the person in the cloak got close enough, he attacked the guards using his walking stick like a staff.

The person in the cloak was a good fighter. He still took several minutes to defeat the two guards. When the first guard had been knocked out, the person's hood fell off as he fought the second guard. Aldous was surprised to see that it was Alden who was the person under the cloak. When the battle was over, Alden stood between the unconscious bodies of the two guards. Alden looked around before putting his hood back up. He bent over and went back to using the staff as a walking stick.

"King Aldous?" Alden's voice was soft as if he was worried that he followed the wrong set of guards. Aldous stood up and stepped out of the shadows.

"I am here," Aldous said.

"Good," Alden said, "King Casimir is here in the city. He needs all the information you have been able to gather. And he may need your help in defeating Garibold."

"Where is he?" Aldous asked.

"Staying at a house," Alden answered, "I am supposed to find you and show you the way."

"We need to get my belongings first," Aldous said, "Follow me and then you can show me where King Casimir is."

"Very well," Alden said. Aldous went to the entrance of the alley and looked out. There were no guards in sight. Aldous left the alley with Alden following behind him.

Aldous took the shortest route that he knew to the alley and his hiding spot. Once they were in the alley, Aldous dug the sack out of his hiding spot. Once he had the sack he turned back to Alden. Out of the corner of his eye, Aldous thought he saw Jasper hiding in the collapsed building watching them. Aldous hoped that Jasper would have the sense to stay where he was and not follow them.

Alden led the way out of the alley and down the street. Aldous followed him away from the poor section of town. They went passed the market place and part way into the merchant class section. Alden finally stopped at a house in the merchant class neighbourhood. This house looked like all the rest of the houses. Alden went up to the door and knocked. A servant opened the door and let Alden and Aldous inside the house. Based on the decorations in the hall of the house, Aldous guessed the owner was in the import and export business. The servant went off to do whatever, leaving Alden and Aldous in the hall. Alden headed down the hall, leaving Aldous the only choice of following him. At the end of the hall was a set of stairs. Alden went up and Aldous followed. At the top of the stairs was another hall. Alden went half way down this hall before stopping at a door and knocking. There was a muffled response. Alden opened the door and Aldous followed him inside. Casimir was standing over a table that had a map on it. Tybalt was sitting on a chair that was against the far wall and one of his warriors was sitting in a chair beside the door. Alden closed the door behind Aldous.

"I am glad Alden found you so quickly," Casimir said, "We arrived yesterday, but a messenger has arrived this morning that Prince Garibold is breaking the negotiations off over some trifle that my diplomat committed."

"Jarlath has been looking for any reason to break off the negotiations," Aldous said.

"The army is set to attack by the end of this week," Casimir said, "That means we need to Prince Garibold out of power before then."

"Is Jarlath responsible for all of this?" Tybalt asked.

"Yes," Aldous answered, "My son in his stupidity has decided that he does not care to rule the kingdom and he lets himself be a puppet to Jarlath. Jarlath is more than happy to oblige."

"I would too if I was going to be handed a kingdom on a platter," Tybalt said, "Especially since he did a nice job of getting you out of the way."

"Yes," Aldous said, "Fortunately, Jarlath is very busy looking at the bigger picture. He has yet to notice the small things."

"Merchant Zenas has been kind enough to let us use his house," Casimir said, "And borrow a map of the castle that he has, not that there is much detail on the map. But from what I can tell there is only one way into the castle."

"There is a way in to the castle?" Aldous asked.

"This is your castle," Casimir answered, "Should you not have known about it?"

"There have been many ways found in and out of the castle," Aldous answered, "So far the only ones that have been successfully navigated are the main entrances."

"This map had a door here at the side of the castle," Casimir said, pointing to a spot on the map. Aldous came close enough to see the map.

"There is a door there," Aldous said, "It leads to a place where the castle and city wall come together. I have been told that the king, that ruled this kingdom before it became Proster, loved that door."

"It leads outside the city?" Alden asked, "That is foolish to have. Then anyone could get in."

"It is locked and barred from the inside," Aldous said, "That was done after a servant went out it and fell the hundred and some metres to their death."

"That door is not an option then," Casimir said.

"I can get us in," Aldous said, "through the main gate."

"How?" Casimir asked.

"With help from one of the servants that is inside the castle," Aldous answered, "She has been bringing me information for the last month. She can be trusted and she would be willing to take the risk."

"That is a good plan," Alden said.

"Or she could open the side gate," Tybalt said, "We avoid all the guards at the main gate until we have taken out Jarlath and taken Garibold out of power."

"That sounds like the better plan," Casimir said.

"I can get her to do that," Aldous said.

"Since you have been here for a month gathering it, what other information could be useful?" Casimir asked.

"Most of the army was gathered by giving them the option between joining the army and rotting in the dungeons," Aldous said, "None of them are particularly loyal to Jarlath or Garibold. None of the nobles will defend either of them. Garibold holds court almost every day of the week. And there are cases for every one of those days. Servants from the castle are sent to get any supplies that are needed, but there is no pattern to when they come. The servants in the castle are minimal and all are overworked. The only day that Garibold does not hold court is Fridays. I am told that he and Jarlath lock themselves in the throne room on Fridays and discuss their plans. And neither of them will be going out to the battlefield when Jarlath orders the attack on Lithimin."

"We go in the side gate on Friday," Tybalt said, "Catch them by surprise and take them out before they realize what is happening."

"Friday is cutting things a little close," Casimir said.

"But this is Tuesday," Tybalt said, "Given that the servant that is giving Aldous information does not come to talk to him regularly, we could be lucky not to have to wait until next week when it is too late."

"What do you think, King Aldous?" Casimir asked.

"Friday is a good day," Aldous answered.

"Are you prepared to fight your own son?" Casimir asked.

"After what I have seen I have to fight him, but I do not want him dead," Aldous answered, "However, I need a day or two to get ready for the battle."

"Merchant Zenas is willing to give you a room until it is time to attack," Casimir said.

"I accept the offer," Aldous said.

"Good," Casimir replied, "There is still some planning that has to happen now that we have a day and an idea of which entrance."

"I will have to go see whether the servant is visiting," Aldous said, "But I have to go alone."

"You are not a prisoner," Casimir replied, "You are free to come and go as you wish."

"Yes," Aldous said, "But I would rather not be followed. It makes my sources of information disappear."

"You have my word that you will not be followed," Casimir said.

"Thank you," Aldous said.

"I will show you to the room reserved for you," Alden said, "Then you can leave you stuff there before you leave."

Aldous nodded. Alden led him out of the room and down the hall. They went up the second staircase and to the third door along this hall. Alden opened it and stepped aside. Aldous entered the room. It was well furnished and looked very comfortable. Alden left. Aldous placed the sack on the bed. Aldous carefully took out the books and placed them on the table beside the bed. Then he carefully took out the armour piece by piece and, as he took out each piece, he placed it in the appropriate position on his bed. When all the armour had been taken out of the bag and placed on the bed, it looked like a metal skeleton lay there. Aldous pulled the medallion out of his shirt.

"Saint Milon," Aldous said, "I have learned your teachings for the last five years. Each one demands that peace be a factor in everything that I do. I hope you will bless this armour for this last battle in which I hope to create a lasting peace. For after this battle, you have my oath that it will never be worn into another battle of any kind." Aldous kissed the medallion. Then he tucked it back in to his shirt and left the room.

There was no one outside waiting for him. Aldous went down to the main door and outside. He went back the way that Alden had brought him. He went passed the market place to the street where Odoric's bakery was. Opening the door Aldous stepped inside. Most of the shelves were empty and Odoric was not behind the counter.

"Odoric," Aldous called. After a moment, Odoric came out of the back of the shop.

"There were rumours that you had been arrested," Odoric looked relieved that Aldous was standing there.

"I was chased out of the market place by some guards," Aldous replied, "It took me a little while to lose them."

"It is a relief to hear that you got away," Odoric said.

"The castle needed supplies?" Aldous asked.

"This morning," Odoric answered, "Faye is in the back right now. She was worried."

"I need to speak with her," Aldous said. Odoric lifted up the piece of counter so that Aldous could pass. Aldous went passed Odoric and into the back. Faye was sitting on the only chair in the kitchen. She got up and hugged Aldous went he got close enough.

"I was terrified that you were gone," Faye said when she released him.

"I am fine," Aldous said, "But I need your help again and this time it will be more dangerous than what I have asked before."

"Anything," Faye said.

"I need you to open the side gate on Friday," Aldous said, "So that King Casimir and I can get inside and confront Garibold and Jarlath in the throne room with as little violence as possible. Can you do that?"

"Of course," Faye said, "This is what I have been waiting for."

"Good," Aldous said, "But I also do not want you to tell anyone about it or about me coming. Any kind of word to anyone could bring the army down on King Casimir and I."

"I will not tell anyone," Faye promised.

"Good," Aldous said, "Once you have let us in I want you to go back to what you should have been doing and you need to stay out of the throne room. The fewer people that are in there the fewer Jarlath will try to harm."

Faye nodded.

"Good," Aldous said. He kissed her forehead. "You leave first."

Faye nodded before picking up her bag and going back out front. Aldous waited until he heard the door open and close. Before going back out front, Odoric lifted the counter to let him through.

"You would not happen to have two loaves of bread left after the castle's take out order, would you?" Aldous asked Odoric.

"Of course, I do," Odoric's face broke in to a smile. He wrapped up the two loaves of bread. "For my king I have only the best."

"I am not returned to the throne yet," Aldous said as he took out the money to pay for the bread.

"No," Odoric acknowledged, "But I am hoping that when you do that there will be space in the castle for the baker of the best bread in the kingdom."

"It is not the baker I am worried about," Aldous said, "It is the rest of the positions which I will have to find people to fill after the reports of how empty the castle has become."

"Your bread," Odoric held out the two loaves.

"Thank you, Odoric," Aldous said, taking the loaves, "I may not be back for several days. Do not worry."

Odoric's face turned serious again and he nodded. Aldous left the bakery. He went down the street until he came to an alley way and he went inside. He went far enough that he could not be seen by any passing guards.

"Jasper?" Aldous asked out loud. Jasper came out of the shadows near by.

"Ralston, what is going on?" Jasper asked.

"Something very important to me," Aldous answered, "I do not want you to be following me."

"I know," Jasper said, "But I want to know what is going on. And everyone else is busy. Uria has been keeping Leander busy with reading and numbers."

Aldous sat down with his back against the wall. Jasper sat down beside him.

"What is happening?" Jasper asked looking up at Aldous.

"King Casimir of Lithimin has asked for my help in removing Prince Garibold from the throne," Aldous answered.

"Why?" Jasper asked.

"Because Prince Garibold is my son," Aldous answered, "And he thinks Prince Garibold will listen to me when he will not listen to anyone else."

"Does that mean you will get everyone's parents out of prison?" Jasper asked.

"I will try," Aldous answered.

"I wish my parents were just in prison," Jasper said.

"What happened to them?" Aldous asked.

"A guard tried to take my mother away," Jasper answered, "And my father refused to let her be taken. I was hiding and the guards did not see me. The guard killed my father in anger over what he had done. And then the guard dragged my mother away. But my mother was found only a street away. She had gotten the guard's knife and had put it through her chest. Chrissy made sure they had a proper burial before taking me in. I was the first she took in. The rest she took in as their parents were taken away and put in prison."

"Do you believe me when I say that I am Prince Garibold's father?" Aldous asked.

"Yes," Jasper answered. Aldous could see that he spoke the truth.

"Then you will believe my promise to you," Aldous said, "I promise that when I am back in the castle, a room will be made up for you and you can live there with me."

"As long as I can visit Leander when he has time," Jasper said.

"That will not be a problem," Aldous replied, "However, until the time I can fulfill that promise you need to stay near Chrissy's house."

"Okay," Jasper said. He looked disappointed.

"But you can take some bread with you," Aldous said holding out the two loaves of bread. Jasper smiled a little at that as he accepted the bread.

"How long?" Jasper started to ask.

"By Friday night it will all be over," Aldous answered.

"Okay," Jasper said. He stood up and went down the alleyway in the direction of Chrissy's house. Aldous watched him go. Aldous continued to sit there for several more minutes before finally getting to his feet. Aldous felt as if old age had suddenly crept in to his bones and decided that it was a nice place to stay. The day a king had to remove his son from the throne is never a day that a king wants to see when the crown is placed on his head. And Aldous had not had to fight any battles in five years. But somehow he knew that when he went in to this battle the strength would be there to help him win. For one thing he had the element of surprise as well as another king and the strong belief that he could win. Aldous hunched over in usual way though he wanted to stand tall as he walked back to the merchant's house.

# PLANS ARE MADE AND THEY PREPARE FOR BATTLE

Aldous did not bother to knock before entering. There was no one in the hall. Aldous went down the hall and up the stairs. He knocked on the door that was Casimir's planning room. The door was opened. The warrior that had been sitting by the door stood there. He opened the door enough to let Aldous inside. Then he closed the door and sat back down in the chair.

"Anything?" Casimir asked from where he was sitting at the table with the map of the castle on it.

"A little bit," Aldous answered.

"Why do you not take a seat?" Casimir asked, "Then Tybalt can tell us the plan that he has rolling over in his head and we can figure out how to improve it."

"The servant that is helping me with information said that she can open the gate for us," Aldous said as he sat down in the chair across from Casimir. Tybalt picked up his chair and set it at the third corner around the table.

"That is good," Tybalt said.

"And that is the end of her involvement," Aldous said.

"Understandable," Casimir replied.

"What time do Jarlath and Prince Garibold shut themselves up in the throne room?" Tybalt asked.

"Shortly after breakfast," Aldous answered.

"Good," Tybalt said, "How many guards are likely to be between the side gate and the throne room?"

"There will be two inside the side gate," Aldous said, "Perhaps two more at the door from the court yard into the castle. If we stay away from the main hallways, we should not meet any more until we reach the door to the throne room. But if we attract the attention of any of the guards or possibly any of the servants, the guards will gather where we are and attack."

"Then, Friday morning, we will get up and arrive at the side gate shortly after breakfast hour. The servant will let us in and we quickly and as quietly as possible knock out the guards at the gate. We will knock the guards out at the side door in the same manner. From there we creep through the halls of the castle until we reach the main doors into the throne room. Then we attack the guards straight on and burst through the doors into the throne room, where we will relieve Prince Garibold of power and restrain Jarlath."

"How many ways are there in to the throne room?" Casimir asked.

"Three," Aldous answered, "The main entrance and the entrance behind the throne that is connected to the study." The others looked at him for several minutes as if they expected him to continue.

"And the third entrance?" Casimir asked finally.

"Is in the floor," Aldous answered, "It goes to the dungeon."

"Directly to the dungeon?" Tybalt asked.

"You pull up the panel, go down the stairs and you are in the dungeon," Aldous answered, "Most people do not even know it is there."

"Then we most definitely have to go through the main entrance," Tybalt said, "We will all go. King Casimir, King Aldous, Alden, me, and my warriors. My warriors and I will be the ones attacking the guards unless an unforeseen situation comes up. However, it would be best if everyone was wearing their armour. It helps the people we are attacking to take us seriously."

"We will have to hide the armour under cloaks from here to inside the castle," Casimir said, "Otherwise we will have to fight our way through the front gate.

Casimir and Tybalt went back and forth discussing the plan in more and more detail. Aldous sat there and answered questions and, on the rare occasion, he added his own suggestions. They discussed the plan to the exact details until Merchant Zenas served supper.

After supper, Aldous went up to the third floor and into the room he had been given the use of. The armour was still spread out on the bed. Aldous went to the chesterfield in the corner of the room. There were several throw pillows on it and a blanket folded up and draped over the back. Aldous unfolded the blanket and curled up on the chesterfield with the blanket covering him. Closing his eyes, Aldous slept.

*Aldous found himself in the throne room of the castle. He was seated on the throne, but he still looked like an old beggar. However, there were a handful of people bowing to him. Aldous recognized Garibold and Theola and Jasper and Odoric and Faye and Alden and Tybalt and Casimir and Jarlath, but he did not recognize the man standing on the red carpet that went up the middle of the room from the door to the dais. The man straightened up. He was medium height, a little on the skinny side as far as build, well fed, brown hair that fell in his eyes, a brown goatee, sparkling blue eyes, and an impish smile.*

*"Who are you?" Aldous asked as the rest of the people disappeared leaving only him and the man in the throne room. Aldous got down off the throne and moved closer to the man.*

*"My name is Milon," the man answered, "In life, I did everything I possibly could to bring peace to people and nations. In death, I was made the saint of peace. I was granted certain abilities that affect the living. I come to you because you believe in peace and creating a peaceful solution to the current war. You asked for my help, but you do not need it if what you have planned goes without fail."*

*"Plans do fail and I did not wish to go back on any of my oaths, vows or promises," Aldous said, "I know my own mind and I know that there are times in which I am not the peaceful person I should be. And I am afraid that my true nature will turn against the man I am trying to become during this situation. I asked for your blessing to keep me from straying from the path of peace I have chosen. You stopped me from war once before and I wish to have that ability available again if I happen to need it."*

*"You are a brave and powerful man," Milon said, "Yet I sense that you are humble, honest, and have a pure heart. I give you my blessing. This will keep you from straying. But, as you wear my symbol into battle, remember that I am a saint, not a god, my abilities are limited."*

*"I understand," Aldous said. Milon faded from sight.*

*"Good luck," Theola's voice was very faint and it was fading away as well. Aldous closed his eyes and spent the rest of the night in a dreamless sleep.*

Aldous opened his eyes. It was morning. He could tell that by the little piece of light that came through the curtains. Aldous got up off the chesterfield and stretched before going to the window. He opened the curtains enough to look out. People were starting to move in other houses. Aldous left the window and went to the door. He stepped out into the hallway. There was no one around. Aldous went down the stairs to the door. He met no one along the way. Aldous left the house. He went to the market place. There were a pair of guards at one end of the market place, but they were watching someone else. Aldous stopped at the pie vender's cart.

"Good morning," the pie vender greeted him as he got a meat pie for Aldous.

"Good morning," Aldous said as he set the money on the counter part of the cart. The pie vender handed him the meat pie.

"Thank you and good day," Aldous said before starting to eat the pie.

"Good day to you too," the pie vender said. Aldous ate the pie as he walked across the market place to the cider vender.

"Good morning," Aldous greeted the cider vender.

"Good morning," the cider vender replied, "Mug or skin?"

"Skin, please," Aldous answered. The cider vender got a skin of cider. He gave it to Aldous as Aldous gave the cider vender the money to pay for it.

"Have a good day," the cider vender said.

"Good day to you as well," Aldous said. He headed off to the next street. Aldous went down it until he came to Odoric's bakery. He went inside. There was a line up of customers. Aldous waited his turn as more people came in behind him.

"Good morning," Odoric said when it was Aldous's turn.

"Good morning," Aldous replied.

"What will you have today?" Odoric asked.

"Two loaves of bread," Aldous answered.

"Very well," Odoric said before getting the loaves of bread and wrapping them up. Aldous gave Odoric the money as Odoric gave him the bread.

"Good day to you," Aldous said.

"Good day to you as well," Odoric replied before turning to the next customer. Aldous left the bakery. He walked to the poor section of the city. Aldous found Jasper sulking in the alleyway.

Aldous left the two loaves of bread and the skin of cider with Jasper before heading back across the city to the house of the merchant Zenas. Since it was lunchtime most of the household and guests were at lunch. Aldous went upstairs rather than into the dining room. He went upstairs to the room he was using. On the table near the chesterfield was a pitcher of water and everything Aldous would need to polish his armour. Aldous took the stuff to polish his armour and started with the piece for the right foot. As he polished, a symbol that matched the one on the medallion he wore appeared on the piece of armour. However, it disappeared once he was finished and put the piece back in its spot on the bed. This happened for each piece of armour as he polished it. Aldous slowly worked his way from the feet up to the top piece of armour. The only piece where the symbol did not disappear was the breastplate, which had never had any adornment on it before.

Polishing his armour took all afternoon, but when Aldous was finished every piece shone as if he had just received it from the blacksmith's shop. When merchant Zenas invited everyone down for supper Aldous was finished and ready for a break.

Aldous went down to the dining room and enjoyed the meal that was set before him. He spoke very little to the others seated near him during the meal and concentrated on the food. When supper was finished the servants cleared the dishes from the table and everyone left the table. Aldous followed when some of the warriors went into the sitting room. He sat down near the fireplace that was not lit. A warrior next to Aldous looked at him.

"I heard that you write histories," the warrior said.

"I did write the history of Proster," Aldous said, "But I have not written much else that is history. I prefer to tell stories instead."

"A story teller?" the warrior said. The rest of the group went quiet and all eyes turned in their direction.

"We do not mind hearing stories, if you do not mind telling us them."

"I do not mind," Aldous replied. He stood up and went to stand in front of the fireplace where everyone could see him without them having to move.

"Once upon a time," Aldous started,

*"There lived a white knight. He travelled far and wide across the land on quests for his king. The king was proud of this white knight and decided*

to give him something for his loyalty. After thinking a while, the king decided that the knight needed a wife to bear him a child and give him an heir. The king sent word out that he was looking for a bride for his loyal knight.

A month later the king received a response. It was a letter arriving by sea captain. It was from a small kingdom that was on an island in the middle of the ocean. There was a princess that was in need of a champion and a husband, and the king had difficulty getting anyone to come and live in the small island kingdom. He would be so grateful for this white knight to be his daughter's husband. The king liked the letter. He had received one other response, but the king did not like it and had worried that it would be the only response. He decided that he had other knights that were getting to be as good as this white knight and they would get better if the white knight was not around to do those jobs. This kingdom needed the white knight more than he did.

So the king sent for the white knight. The white knight arrived in the throne room with the promptness that the king had come to expect from him.

"How can I serve you today?" the white knight asked, bowing low before the king on his throne.

"I received a letter from the king of a small kingdom on an island in the middle of the ocean," the king answered, "And you are my best knight, so it is you I choose to send."

"What sort of help does this king need?" the white knight asked.

"His daughter is in need of a champion," the king answered.

"When do I leave?" the white knight asked.

"I have arranged with the sea captain, who brought the letter, for you to sail with him," the king answered, "The ship is sailing in two days. The captain is leaving for the port tomorrow morning."

"I will go and help this princess," the white knight said as he bowed to the king. Then he left the throne room. From the throne room, he went in search of the sea captain. He found the sea captain drinking and listening to stories in the guard's barracks.

"So, you are the white knight," the sea captain said when he saw the white knight.

"I am," the white knight replied, "The king said that you are leaving for port tomorrow."

"I am," the sea captain said, "Bright and early in the morning. Just before the sun rises in the east."

"I will meet you at that time inside the walls that surround the palace," the white knight said.

"Okay," the sea captain said. The white knight left the guard's barracks and went to his rooms. The rooms were bare, with only the white knight's clothes and armour, and some bare furniture. The white knight did not believe having too much comfort when at the palace. Also he usually took everything that belonged to him when he went on quests. The white knight packed up everything as he usually did.

He was packed and ready when he went to the great hall for supper. He ate with the others, but he was always slightly apart from them socially. This meant that he ate alone in a hall full of people.

When he had finished eating his fill, the white knight went back to his rooms. He immediately lay down on the bed and closed his eyes. He went to sleep immediately just as he had trained himself to do.

He woke up at the time he wanted. It was still dark as he got out of bed. The white knight lit the candle that was beside his bed. He went through some training exercises that made very little noise, but kept him battle ready. When he was finished, he got ready for the journey ahead of him. Once ready, he went down to the stables and readied his horse. The grooms were not awake and so he had to ready his horse himself. He did not mind. He was used to doing things himself. When he had his horse ready, he went out to where he said that he would meet the sea captain. The sea captain had not arrived yet, so the white knight waited.

The sun's light was started to show in the sky when the sea captain came out. He was also leading a horse.

"Are you ready?" the sea captain asked as he stopped to mount his horse.

"I am," the white knight answered as he mounted his horse.

"Then we are off," the sea captain said.

Together they left the palace walls. Off through the fields of the kingdom they went. They rode all day, only resting when the sea captain needed to stop. The white knight ate when they stopped for lunch and waited patiently for the sea captain to be ready to move on for all the rest of the stops. The sea captain always seemed surprised every time the white knight turned down stopping to rest. When evening fell the white knight and the sea captain had to stop for the night at a roadside inn. The white knight ate with the sea captain in the main room of the inn, but after he was finished eating the white knight went to his room to sleep rather than staying up with the sea captain to drink and listen to people talk.

As was his routine, the white knight rose while it was still dark and did his exercises before making sure that his belongings were packed and going down to the stable and getting his horse ready. The sea captain arrived in the stables as the first light appeared over the horizon. And they headed off.

They arrived in the port city around noon. The sea captain led the way to a stable that bought and sold horses. Both the sea captain and the white knight sold their horses. The white knight did this after the sea captain explained how long it would take to get to this island kingdom and how long it would take to get back. After they had sold the horses the sea captain led the way to a drinking establishment near the wharf. The food was edible, but it most likely that people went for the drink. The white knight ate the food, but left the drink. The sea captain shook his head at the white knight's behaviour before taking the white knight's drink for himself. Once he was finished eating the white knight waited patiently while the sea captain had one more drink after the two he had while eating lunch.

When the sea captain was finally finished, they left the drinking establishment. The sea captain led the way down the wharf to a large cargo ship. The crew were doing as the first mate was ordering. The sea captain and the white knight went up the gangplank. The sea captain conferred with the first mate while one of the sailors showed the white knight to his bunk. His bunk was the only guest cabin the ship had. The white knight put his belongings in the trunk that was attached to the bed that was attached to both the wall and the floor.

"We will be leaving soon," the sailor told the white knight before leaving the cabin. The white knight looked around the cabin and decided that it was a good place to sleep. It was as bare as his rooms in the palace.

He would be comfortable here. Once he had closed the lid of the trunk he went back up to the deck of the ship. All the sailors were busy: the first mate was giving orders, and the sea captain was not around. The white knight found a place near the railing that over looked the wharf. He watched people come and go along the wharf. They went about their business.

Finally, the sea captain came back on deck and gave the order to set sail. The white knight watched the flurry of activity at the order. The gangplank was raised and the ship was untied from the wharf. The white knight could feel the ship moving away from the wharf and dry land. He had never been to sea, but he went because the king ordered him to. If you had asked him whether he was afraid, he would not have known the answer, as his only thoughts were to serve the king.

The white knight watched the port city as the ship moved farther and farther away from it. Slowly it became smaller until it was only a speck in the distance and then it was gone from sight. The white knight took to watching the water and all the creatures he could see near the surface.

When supper was served, the white knight ate what provisions that he was offered, though they hardly looked edible. When he was finished supper he went down to the cabin he had been given the use of and after lying down on the bed he went to sleep.

The white knight woke to the moving of the ship. It seemed to be moving more than the day before. The white knight got out of bed and found it difficult to keep his balance to do his exercises, but he persevered through them. When he was finished the white knight went up on to the deck. The only people on deck were the sailors on watch, everyone else was still asleep. The white knight went to where he had been standing the day before and stayed there watching. As he watched the darkness faded away and the sunrise was perfect. The only place the white knight had seen a more beautiful sunrise had been the top of the tallest mountain when he had gone up there in search of a dragon.

The white knight went down to where everyone ate when others started to wake up. There he received similar food to what he had been given the night before for supper. The white knight ate without comment and went back on deck. The sails were full and the ship was going a very good speed. And the white knight saw the occasional sea creature.

When suppertime came the white knight went down and ate supper. If it had bothered him to eat alone when at the palace it might have bothered him to eat alone here on a ship full of people, but neither bothered him. After he was finished eating he went to his room for the night.

Several more days went by as the first one had. One day the sea captain approached the white knight.

"We still have three more weeks before we get there," the sea captain told the white knight. The white knight nodded but continued to watch some sort of sea animal jumping in the distance.

"If you get bored or have any questions, my crew is willing to share their knowledge," the sea captain said. The white knight glanced at the sea captain.

"Will there be trouble?" the white knight asked.

"Usually about the second week out we run in to large groups of storms," the sea captain answered, "That is the only trouble between here and there. No pirates sail these waters. But when we hit the storms it might be a good idea to know something about sailing so that you can help out."

"I will learn what I can," the white knight said.

"I just thought I would give you a warning," the sea captain said before turning and walking away.

The white knight, however, spent the rest of the day watching the sea life around him.

The next day the white knight found one of the oldest sailors on the ship who was willing to talk to him and teach him whatever he wanted to know. The white knight followed him and learned everything he could from the man. The old sailor was not sure about the white knight, but by the end of that day had decided that the white knight was on his way to becoming a fine sailor. The white knight and the old sailor worked together for that week. At the end of it, the sea captain watched as the white knight helped around the ship like a seasoned sailor would have. And he did a very good job, even if there were still certain things that he still was not sure about. This was a pleasant surprise to the sea captain as most passengers only get enough information to get through the storms. But since the white knight was willing, the sea captain was more than willing to allow him to work as a sailor.

Another week went by with the white knight taken in by the sailors. They were willing to talk with him and tell him something if he needed to know. The white knight even found himself not eating alone. He was included in the conversation. The white knight found himself enjoying talking to others during meal times. And the fact that they left him to his own schedule made things even better. He also found that his exercises got easier, not only keeping his balance as he did them, but also in doing the exercises themselves. The exercise of being a sailor agreed with his body.

On the morning that ended the second week he arrived on deck while it was still dark. The watches were in their places, but something about the air felt heavier. The white knight figured that it was the storms coming in. He was just about to go to the spot where he had watched the creatures for the first several days when he heard someone singing. It was a beautiful female voice. The white knight tried to figure out where it was coming from, but only found it to be coming over the water.

He was still standing there when the old sailor came above deck.

"That is a mermaid's call," the old sailor said, "Most do not believe they are out there, but it is true. It is like a siren's call. It wraps itself around a man's heart and makes him long for something that will never be his. The mermaid's call is not a call to bring a man to danger though, it is to warn a man away from it."

"It is warning us about the storm," the white knight said.

"Most first timers can not hear that," the old sailor said, "They get so wrapped up in the song that they do not understand it."

"It has a voice that cries a warning," the white knight replied, "I recognize that."

"I suppose you would," the old sailor said, "Best get ready for a bad storm." The old sailor patted the white knight on the shoulder and went off to where he needed to be. The white knight looked around and saw that it was still dark because of the dark storm clouds, not because it was still night. The white knight turned to go to the position the sea captain told him to be in if a storm hit. But the white knight found himself glancing over his shoulder out at the sea before his feet started in the right direction.

Perhaps the old sailor was right about the song wrapping around the heart, the white knight thought. He had never had this experience before, but

113

*something had changed. He just could not tell what. For one thing, that song was still going around in his head even though he could no longer hear the mermaid singing. And second, he wanted to meet the mermaid and see if she was a beautiful as her voice. These thoughts were not ones that the white knight would normally entertain and, even now, there were parts of his brain that told him that this way of thinking was a slippery slope to a place he had vowed never to be. Yet somehow, the more he tried to put the thoughts about the mermaid out of his head the more those thoughts pushed through.*

*Water hitting his face woke him out of the thoughts that were pulsing around his head. It was starting to rain and it was raining hard. In minutes, the white knight was soaked to the skin and the deck was slippery. The rain was the only problem for several hours, which meant that the trouble was not too bad yet. But shortly after noon, the wind picked up and was making the waves choppy. As night approached, thunder and lightening were added. The white knight took shifts with everyone else as the storm continued the next day and the day after.*

*It was the fourth day of storms that everyone was starting to be more enthusiastic because the fourth day was usually the last day of the storms. After this, it should be smooth sailing to the island kingdom. But the fourth day brought harder rain, stronger winds and all round worse weather. All men were instructed to tie themselves to the ship after the first man had to be rescued from being washed overboard. The white knight had spent a good part of the day below deck, but a sailor had been brought down after being slammed into something. The sailors that brought the sailor below gave the white knight the rope that had kept the man on board the ship. The white knight tied it around himself and then went on deck to help out. He had been out there for an hour when a large wave washed over the ship. The white knight felt his feet lift off the deck of the ship and the wave took him over the side and into the water. The white knight saw some others in the water with him. He followed their example in using the rope tied to him to haul himself towards the ship. The white knight was close to the ship when another wave came over the ship and swept him further away. This time the rope securing him to the ship snapped. The waves started to toss him around like a plaything. The white knight tried to swim back to the ship, but the waves were stronger. He soon found himself tiring. He forced himself to swim harder, but it did not help. The white knight stopped trying to swim for the ship and just tried to stay afloat in hopes that he would drift out of the storm.*

*As he tired the white knight found himself slipping under the water. This would wake him up enough that he would try to stay above water again. He was a very strong person, but the white knight eventually lost the fight. He was not sure how long he had stayed afloat or when he sank into unconsciousness, but he did."*

Aldous stopped as he noticed the men were starting to yawn.

"And I will finish the tale tomorrow night," Aldous said, "Good night."

A chorus of good nights followed Aldous as he left the room and went upstairs.

Aldous went back up to his room and curled up on the chesterfield again with the blanket covering him. He thought of the sword he had lost in the battle where he had last worn his armour. He was not sure what happened to it. Aldous hoped that someone would be willing to loan him a sword for the battle. Armour without a sword did not feel right even to a man of peace.

Aldous closed his eyes and fell in to a dreamless sleep.

Aldous woke as he had the day before. The view outside his window was similar to the day before. Aldous left the house as he had the day before, not meeting anyone else on his way out. Then he turned toward the market place and followed his usual routine of buying a meat pie and a mug of cider. There were no guards around the market place today so Aldous was able to enjoy the leisure of sitting on the low wall and enjoying them. Then he walked to Odoric's bakery. Odoric was behind the counter, but his shelves had been cleaned off, except for the occasional baked good that remained. There were no customers to wait in line behind today.

"Good morning," Aldous greeted Odoric.

"Good morning," Odoric said, "Faye is in the back." Odoric lifted the counter. Aldous went passed him and into the kitchen. Faye was seated on the only chair.

"Good morning," Aldous greeted her.

"When do I need to be there to open the gate?" Faye asked.

"Open the side gate shortly after the breakfast hour on Friday," Aldous answered.

"Okay," Faye said with a nod, "I can do that."

"Have there been any changes up at the castle over the last few days?" Aldous asked.

"No," Faye shook her head as she looked thoughtful, "Unless you count the fact that Jarlath seems to be trying to convince Prince Garibold that he should get married so that there will be an heir to the throne if he dies."

"That is not much of a change," Aldous said, "That is just Jarlath getting to the next stage of his plan."

"Any woman would have to be strong to not be affected by Jarlath's love for power and Prince Garibold's disregard for his proper position," Faye said.

"I doubt that Jarlath would be picking such woman for Garibold to marry," Aldous said.

"There are more than a few noblewoman that would play whatever game Jarlath wants if they get to marry Prince Garibold," Faye said, "I have seen that much. They all seem too foolish in their attempt at gaining his attention. I do not know what kind of woman he is looking for, but he has not been swayed by Jarlath to marry one of the noblewomen that keep fawning over him."

"Then he does have some sense in his head," Aldous said, "That is good, I thought he had lost it all."

"Will everything be all right?" Faye asked.

"Of course it will be all right," Aldous answered her, "I do not like to plan things that do not turn out as I had hoped."

"But you were caught by King Casimir when you went in to battle with him," Faye said.

"There was no fight," Aldous admitted, "I had a vision of what my men's future would be if they did not die in battle. I made a choice to save their lives. I exchanged myself for their lives and King Casimir honoured that and did them no harm. It was the right decision at the time, though I thought Garibold would be a better king than he turned out to be. Do you understand?"

"Yes," Faye nodded, though she looked very thoughtful.

"Perhaps you should think on it," Aldous said, "But the whole attack will hinge on you opening the side gate for us on Friday."

"I will be there," Faye promised.

"Good," Aldous said. He turned and went back out front. Odoric lifted the piece of counter and Aldous went through before turning back to Odoric.

"Could you do me a favour?" Aldous asked.

"Certainly," Odoric answered.

"Can you deliver my two loaves of bread to a Chrissy that lives in the poor section of the city?" Aldous asked, "I would do it myself, but I have an appointment to keep."

"I can deliver them," Odoric said.

"Thank you," Aldous said as he gave Odoric the money for the two loaves of bread, "Have a good day."

"You have a good day as well," Odoric said. Aldous left Odoric's bakery and headed back to Merchant Zenas's house.

After having to take a few detours to avoid patrols Aldous reached the house just as lunch was being served. He joined the rest of the household and guests in the dining room for lunch. Though he spent more time talking with the people next to him than eating, Aldous found that he enjoyed himself.

After lunch, Aldous was directed to a room that the servant referred to as the bath room. Inside was a tub filled with warm water as well as a stack of fresh clothes, which had been made so that they would fit under his armour and he could still wear them as clothing until then. Aldous stripped and got into the tub of water.

By the time he had gotten out, he had used up the bar of soap that he had been given. But he was clean. After drying himself off, Aldous put on the new clothes. Then he presented himself to the servant who would cut his hair for him. Aldous gave the servant directions and the servant followed them exactly. It was only when the servant was done and cleaning up the chair that Aldous went back up to his room and stood before the mirror. The man who stood there had no scholarly stoop or beggar's beard. He had had his hair cut to shoulder length, which, though now white, looked dignified. He also had his beard trimmed to be short enough not to get in his soup, but long enough that it was dignified as well. With a clean face and fresh clothing, Aldous looked like he might deserve the title of king again. He certainly felt good about himself and the battle that would take place the next day.

Aldous left his room and went down to the second floor. He knocked on the door to the room that Casimir was using as a study and war room. The door was opened by the same warrior that had opened it before. The warrior let him in before sitting back down. Casimir and Tybalt were looking at the map spread out on the table. They were waiting for him so that they could do a run through of the plan again. Aldous went to the chair that made the third corner around the table. Casimir looked up at him before he sat down.

"You certainly look like a king now," Casimir commented. Tybalt looked up at Aldous and nodded his approval.

"I only hope I look that good when I get to your age," Casimir added.

"Life as a beggar is not as bad as it seems once you remove the dirt," Aldous said as he sat down, "But we should get on with going over the plans for tomorrow. Are we not having the others joining us?" Aldous looked around the room, except for Casimir and Tybalt, the only the warrior was by the door.

"Alden is doing a short training exercise with them in the fighting area behind the house," Tybalt replied, "They will be here shortly."

Aldous nodded. Casimir and Tybalt went back to what they what been discussing and Aldous sat there listening.

A few minutes later, there was a knock at the door and Alden opened the door before the warrior could get up to open it.

"Come in," Casimir told Alden. Alden came in and found a seat. The rest of Tybalt's warriors followed him.

Tybalt took charge of the group once everyone was settled and he explained every detail of the plan to the group.

By the time he was finished and had answered the few questions that people had, a servant had come to inform them that supper was ready. Everyone filed out, except Aldous, Casimir and Tybalt. Only after everyone else had exited the room did they get up and follow. Once again, Aldous found himself enjoying talking to the people on either side of him during the meal.

After supper, Aldous joined the warriors in the sitting room again. This evening more of them had chosen to join them.

"You promised us the rest of the story," the warrior that had invited Aldous to start the story said.

"I did," Aldous said as he went to the stand in front of the fireplace.

"I cannot wait to find out what happens to the white knight," someone near the back of the crowd said. He was told to shut up and everyone focused on Aldous.

"The white knight had slipped under the choppy waves of the sea and into unconsciousness," Aldous started,

*"The white knight coughed and spit up seawater. He fell from his side onto his stomach as he coughed up more seawater. When he was finished coughing the white knight lifted his head and looked around him. The sun was shining down on him, and the beach, the white knight was on was mostly golden sand with some rocks, but the white knight could see trees not*

that far away. He slowly sat up. He was sitting in the middle of a beach with the sea not that far away. The white knight might have thought he washed up on this spot, but there were drag marks in the sand. It looked like someone had dragged a large fish, human sized, across the sand. The white knight got to his feet and looked around. Just a few feet in front of him was a grassy area with several trees, at least one of which was fruit bearing. And beyond that was another beach and then the sea. It was not a very big island. The white knight turned and looked out at sea, but there was no sign of a ship or other landmass in sight.

The white knight sat back down in the sand. Partially out of dizziness and partially out of not being sure what to do next. He had nothing here. All his belongings were in the trunk of the ship and there was not much on the island.

As he was sitting there, the white knight could hear someone start to sing. He looked up and around. He looked on the island and out to sea. But the white knight could not see the person that was singing. It was a sweet song, like that of someone that was in love. Those sweet notes turned the white knight's heart. Though he had never been in love he could feel it as if he was the lover in the song. Sitting there, listening, the white knight wondered why he had been so wrapped up in his loyalty to the king that he could not fall in love with a woman. It felt like he had missed something that was very important in life.

As suddenly as it had come, the song ended. The white knight expected that the song would leave him feeling empty, but it did not. It left him feeling like the first chance he got, he would fall in love. However, there was still one part of his head that told him that falling in love would break his vows.

The white knight got up and went up the beach to where the sand was. He looked at the fruit in the tree and decided that it looked similar to something he had watched the king eat. He picked a piece off and bit into it. It tasted sweet, so he ate the rest of the fruit. Looking around, he found branches that he could use to make a shelter and started construction. By the time night had fallen, he was asleep under the shelter he had made.

The next morning, he had gone to the water's edge to wash up and the white knight found a fish lying on the sand. It had been killed and had not just washed up on the sand. Once he had washed up, the white knight built *a fire. He cooked the fish over it and ate it for breakfast. He called out a thank you to the mermaid, though he could not see her, before going back to the grassy area. He spent time doing various exercises.*

*When he had taken a break from the exercises and was sitting on the grass eating a piece of fruit, the white knight heard the singing start again. This time the song sounded more broken hearted. Again the emotions from the song filled the white knight's heart and he understood the feelings. And though the song was sad, he wished he had not missed out on that part of life. Again there was part of his mind that told him that doing such a thing would mean breaking his vows.*

*The singing stopped just as it had started. The white knight got up and continued his exercises even with thoughts that he tried to push away coming back. For supper, the white knight had another piece of fruit before going to sleep under his shelter.*

*This pattern continued for several more days. Each day had a different song that conjured up a different emotion for the white knight. Each emotion he had never felt before and he was sorry for the missed chance. But there was always that thought in the back of his head that having such feelings would have meant breaking his vows.*

*On the morning of the fifth day, the white knight ate the fish left for him by the mermaid before going back to the grassy area. Instead of doing his exercises, the white knight sat down in the grass and meditated.*

*When the white knight had just been a squire, the knight that was doing the training asked him what kind of knight he wanted to become. Of course, the knight he was training with had been a white knight so he had answered that he wanted to be a white knight. Now, he was beginning to understand the sigh that man gave. It was not out of relief, but out of an understanding that the boy did not have. Being a white knight was the hardest, though it always looked like the easiest. The vow to become a white was long and very strict. To become a grey or black knight required a vow of less restrictions. A white knight was supposed to be pure at all times. That meant helping anyone they came across that needed help, avoiding lust and temptation, not having much for material possessions, and of course swearing loyalty to only one king. The white knight had done all of these for many years and it had brought him nothing. A saddlebag of possessions, no* emotional attachments at all, and eating alone in a hall full of people were the only things he had in this life. Very few understood what being a white knight meant and they were as boring to talk to as a white knight is.

The white knight's teacher had seen great potential in him and he was sorry to see it all wasted on being a white knight. But the white knight had known a few who had to change their colours due to events that happened. They did not have to take a new vow; they just had to change the colour they wore and act under the restrictions of the new vow. The white knight knew he could never live under the restrictions of the black knight. But perhaps he could go grey; the restrictions were exactly as he had decided he would like to live. It would shock people when they saw the change in his colour, but most would accept it. The king might have a problem with it, but the knight would see what the king said only if he ever got back there.

He had sat down a white knight and now he stood up as a grey knight. He ate a fruit from the tree as he walked around the island. He might have to do his exercises tomorrow, but as a grey knight it was not required of him to do them daily. When the grey knight got back to the side of the island, a ship appeared on the horizon. The grey knight built up the fire he had started that morning. Since it had not gone out completely, it was easy to build it up again. The grey knight watched the ship come closer. Finally it came as close to the island as it could and put down the anchor. A smaller boat was lowered and started toward the island. As it got closer, the grey knight recognized the sea captain and the old sailor.

"We thought you had died in the storm," were the first words out of the sea captain's mouth once they had gotten to the grey knight where he had waded out to them.

"I was saved and brought here," the grey knight answered. They helped him into the boat and got it moving back to the ship.

"You got lucky then," the old sailor said, "Most of the time, mermaids let you die."

"I do not know why, I just know that something saved me," the grey knight said.

"Well, from here it should be smooth sailing," the sea captain said.

"Good," the grey knight said. Soon they were back at the ship. The crew was happy to see the grey knight and he was happy to see them.

He surprised them all at supper when he stayed to talk to them after he finished eating, but the grey knight told himself that he was allowed to do so now that he was a grey knight. And over the next few days, he surprised himself and others in his flexibility. The crew quickly chalked it up to surviving the storm, but the grey knight knew that was through the mermaid's song.

Five days after rescuing the grey knight, the ship docked at the island kingdom. The sea captain sent word to the palace that the knight had arrived. The grey knight got himself presentable as well as gathering his belongings, before going up on deck and waiting for someone to come from the palace to escort him there. While on deck, he said good-bye to the crew members, especially the old sailor. Finally an older knight and a squire arrived at the ship to escort the grey knight to the palace. They brought a horse with them. The grey knight said good-bye to the captain and mounted the horse. And the three on horses headed for the palace.

Once they arrived, the grey knight was immediately taken to the throne room. He went and bowed before the king. The king welcomed him and was so happy that his daughter now had a champion. The king went on and on. The grey knight had looked up at the king and his eyes had fallen on the princess. She had long flowing blonde hair, a smooth complexion, pale green eyes, and an aura that said that she would be that beautiful if all she had to wear was a paper bag. The grey knight found himself more than transfixed and all the way to smitten. Out of everything the king said, the grey knight got that there was going to be a tournament and that he was defending the princess from a black knight. And this would all happen tomorrow. The grey knight's only thought as he bowed to the king for the last time before leaving was that he would do anything for the princess and the little half smile she had been giving him.

The grey knight was shown to a small bare cell like room, befitting a white knight. Once the door was closed, the grey knight sighed and put his belongings on the floor. Then he went off to find the kitchen. He found it without much difficulty. And he managed to talk to cook in to giving him some food. Then he took the food and found the tallest tower, where he sat and ate. He surveyed the whole island from his vantage point. It was a very *nice kingdom. When it started to get dark, the grey knight went back to his room and went to bed.*

*The next morning, he joined everyone else in the great hall for breakfast. After breakfast, a squire joined the grey knight as he got ready for the tournament. The squire showed him where everything was as well as pointing out which horse he could use. The squire stayed to help the grey knight prepare for the fight. The grey knight just about sent the squire away, but decided to let the squire help him. A white knight required help from no one but himself; a grey knight, however, is willing to accept help that is offered. Finally, when he was ready, the grey knight went to the tournament grounds. Everything else was set up and the black knight was ready and waiting. The grey knight got in to position. The king called the command that started the tournament.*

*The grey knight won against the black knight. He went to where the king and the princess were seated in a shaded pavilion and bowed before the king.*

*'I proclaim the white knight to be the winner,' the king announced, 'He bested the black knight in all rounds of combat. As agreed upon when this tournament was set my daughter is the prize. And I now present her to the white knight for them to be married this evening.'*

*The grey knight was shocked for a minute before the happiness filled his heart. And from the smile the princess was giving him she was happy about the outcome as well. So they were married that evening as planned. And they lived happily ever after."*

When he was finished, Aldous bowed before leaving the room to the applause. Aldous went up to his room on the third floor. Inside, he curled up on the chesterfield with the blanket covering him and fell asleep.

# THE BATTLE IS SHORT BUT VICTORY GOES TO THE RIGHT SIDE

The sun was not up yet when Aldous woke to the sound of horse's hooves on the street outside the window. Aldous got off the chesterfield and looked out the window. In the little bit of light that there was, he could that the horse was attached to a cart full of goods with a man dressed in merchant clothing sitting in the driver's seat. Aldous let the curtain fall back over the window before turning away.

Listening Aldous could hear other people moving around in other rooms of the house. He decided that he might as well get ready for the day ahead. The person who is supposed to wake him up would probably be here soon and then one of Merchant Zenas's servants would come in to help him put his armour on. Aldous did not like people helping him get into his armour so he might as well get moving.

Aldous went to the basin of water that was on the table in front of the mirror. He washed up. Then he started putting his armour on. Aldous carefully strapped each piece on. Some of the pieces felt too big, but not enough that it would move too much on Aldous. So he was not worried about them too much. The rest fit just as they had five years ago when he had taken them off.

When he was finished, he checked himself in the mirror. Aldous looked like a king ready for battle. The only thing that was missing was the sword that should fill the empty scabbard that hung limply from his hip. Aldous missed the sword that had been given to him. The blacksmith that had made the sword for Aldous had given it the name of Petrina. The name was engraved in the hilt rather than a lot of fancy, but useless, jewels. That is what Aldous liked about the sword: it was practical, not decorative. As king he was given too many things that were useless or bulky because he was king and thus it all must have jewels all over it until it might as well sit in a display case. When Aldous received the throne, he had also received what was known as the king's sword. It weighed twice as much as any other sword in the kingdom and had a thief's dream of jewels embedded in it. Aldous had used a training sword for years until a blacksmith had noticed and made Petrina. Aldous was willing to give the blacksmith almost anything he wanted in return for such as wonderful gift, but the blacksmith refused any offer of payment. However Aldous always sent work his way after that. Aldous missed Petrina.

After taking a deep breath, Aldous left the room. Passing other rooms on the third floor, he could see in a few open doors that Tybalt's warriors were also putting on their armour. Aldous went passed all the rooms on the third floor, went down the staircase to the second floor, and stopped at the open door of the study Casimir was using as a war room. Casimir was standing in the middle of the room as Alden was finishing putting his armour on him. Tybalt was already in his armour and sitting in his usual chair against the one wall of the study.

"Come in," Casimir said when he noticed that Aldous was standing in the doorway. Aldous entered the study and sat down in one of the two chairs that were near the table, which today had been cleaned off.

"Are you ready?" Tybalt asked as Alden finished with Casimir's last piece of armour besides the helmet.

"I am just about ready to do this," Aldous answered Tybalt.

"Just about?" Tybalt asked, "What would help to make you completely ready?"

"I am missing a sword," Aldous answered, "Armour has never been complete without that comforting weight of the sword. I lost my sword five years ago when I was taken prisoner and I did not have enough money to buy myself another one. I had hoped that someone could loan me one."

"I can do better than that," Casimir said. He went to the corner and picked up a cloth bundle. He brought it back to the table.

"Knowing that you would be helping us today, I brought this for you," Casimir said as he unwrapped the cloth. Petrina was the sword that was under the cloth, "Since you are no longer a prisoner of my realm, I feel that it is my duty to return this to you."

"Thank you very much," Aldous said, taking Petrina. He felt the weight of her in his hand and the day got better. Standing up, he slid Petrina into his scabbard and his armour felt right.

"We have a little more than an hour until we are to be at the side gate," Alden reported.

"We need to get moving," Casimir said, "Get everyone ready." Alden bowed to Casimir before leaving the study.

"Now you are ready?" Tybalt asked Aldous.

"Yes," Aldous answered.

"Good," Casimir said, "We need to go." Tybalt stood up and the three of them left the study. They went down the stairs to the first floor. Several of Tybalt's warriors were waiting in the sitting room. Casimir, Aldous and Tybalt went in to the sitting room and waited standing by the fireplace. The rest of Tybalt's warriors filtered into the room as ten minutes passed. Finally,

Alden came into the sitting room with a nod at Casimir that all the warriors were in the sitting room and none were missed.

"Everyone has their route to the castle and knows what to do when we get inside," Tybalt said, "You better remember all that if you want to get in on the fighting. And remember that we wish to do as little harm as possible. Everyone ready?"

"Yes, sir," all the different voices sounded as one.

"Good," Tybalt said, "Let us go. Your orders has already been given to you." The first five warriors went in to the hallway and the front door could be heard to open and close. Alden brought three black cloaks to Casimir, Aldous and Tybalt. Alden helped Casimir put his own. Tybalt took his and put it on. Aldous also put his own cloak on. They covered the armour each man was wearing. Most of the warriors were wearing similar cloaks. Alden went off as the next five warriors left the sitting room and went into the hallway. They rest could be heard leaving as well. Alden came back a moment later with his own cloak on. Casimir led Aldous, Tybalt, Alden and one of Tybalt's warriors into the hallway and out the front door. The neighbourhood was quiet as people were only starting their day and many were eating breakfast.

The group walked through the streets of the capital city. They stuck to shadows where they could and alleyways as much as possible. The twisting and turning snake like progress was slow. At one point, Aldous was not sure he was not lost. However, Casimir and Tybalt seemed to know exactly where they were going. Never underestimate your enemy, Aldous thought watching them, it could cause you more trouble than you think.

Finally they arrived at the alleyway opening that was across the street from the side gate. Several of Tybalt's warriors were already there and waiting. As they stood there, more arrived. It was starting to get close to time for Faye to open the gate. Aldous put his hood up and walked out into the street with his stoop back. Casimir tried to grab him and drag him back into the alley way, but Aldous was moving too fast for him to get a hold. Aldous hobbled across the street to the gate. He sat down at the base of the door while keeping a watch for any guards. No guards came by. Aldous put his ear to the crack in the gate and listened.

"Guarding this gate is terrible," said a male voice that Aldous was sure was one of the guards.

"How long has it been since you have been allowed to go home?" a second male voice asked.

"Five days," the first guard answered, "My wife is trying to convince the neighbours that I have not been sent off and killed in the fighting, that I am still alive and stationed in the city. How about yourself?"

"Six days," the second voice replied, "I am missing my son's third month."

"How many children do you have?" the first guard asked.

"My son is my first one," the second voice answered, "And I never thought that I would be so proud of something so small that spends all its time eating and sleeping. When he is not spitting up, of course. Do you have any children?"

"I might if I was not working the long days that I have been since I got married," the first guard said, "Right now if my wife gets pregnant it is more likely to be someone else's child than mine."

"I am not sure why Prince Garibold needs two guards on every entrance all the time," the second guard said, "When King Aldous was here he would leave these gates open and unguarded. It was much nicer. People came and went all the time. There were only two guards where he went. And those two had four-hour shifts. I would trade five days stuck out here guarding the side gate for four hours of boredom listening to a peasant complaining about his neighbour's cow mooing too loudly any day."

"If Jarlath was not so paranoid about the populace, none of us would be forced to do such long shifts," the first guard said,

"That and sending all but a few of the guards off to fight a war no one wants to fight does not help at all."

"I do not know how well Prince Garibold would do if he did not have Jarlath to rule the kingdom for him," the second guard said, "But it would be nice to find out."

"Did you hear about the rumoured announcement?" the first guard asked.

"The rumour that Prince Garibold has given in to Jarlath and agreed to marry Lord Oren's brainless daughter," the second guard said.

"That one," the first guard said, "Do you think it could be true?"

"With the way that Prince Garibold has been about marriage, I would say no," the second guard answered, "But Jarlath has been wearing his cocky smile all day today. That tells me that he has worn Prince Garibold down enough that Prince Garibold accepted the idea of marriage. With Lord Oren being so willing to support Jarlath, I would believe that Jarlath has arranged things with Lord Oren to marry his daughter off to Prince Garibold. The daughter is probably more than willing to be sold into the marriage."

"Not a good situation all around," the first guard said, "With those two married then Jarlath will have the kingdom to himself. Which probably means that it will three years before I see my wife again."

"Maybe she will think that you did get sent off to fight King Casimir's army in Lithimin and you died there," the second guard said, "She may even remarry so that someone will support her."

"Not likely to happen," the first guard said, "I write her letters and sent them with the kitchen servants when they go to town to get food for the castle. She knows that I am alive and thinking of her. And she gets money from me to support her. I have even received a letter in return."

"Doing that would just make me more homesick and I would desert my post," the second guard, "Seeing my family might be worth it, but I do not want to spend the rest of my life running from my fellow guardsmen."

"Halt!" the first guard demanded, "What do you want?"

"I am expecting a delivery," Faye's voice was recognizable through the crack in the door. Aldous signaled Casimir, Tybalt and Tybalt's warriors to get ready.

"The delivery person cannot come into the court yard," the second guard said.

"I know," Faye replied," But I was hoping that you would be willing to open the gate so that I could see if the person is here already and waiting for me."

"We can do that," the first guard said. Aldous signalled that the gate was about to be opened. Then he got to his feet. Aldous moved back from the gate. The rest of the group came out of the alleyway and over to where he stood. Aldous found himself in the middle of the group, along with the cloaked figures of Casimir and Alden. The gate opened enough for one person would be able to fit through. Two of the warriors slipped inside. The gate was opened a little more a moment later and the rest of the group went inside. One of the warriors stepped away from the group and closed the gate. The two guards were lying knocked out and were being tied up by the first two warriors. Faye stood to one side watching everything. Aldous looked at her. She was searching the hoods for any sign of him. Finally she saw his eyes. He gave her a nod. Then Faye turned and headed off; probably back to what she was supposed to be doing.

The warriors came back to the group and the whole group moved carefully across the side courtyard. When they reached the wall of the castle, they went along it to the corner close where the door they needed to go in was. Once again, two warriors moved around the corner. This time they dragged the guards around the corner to where the rest of the group was and out of sight of the rest of the courtyard. The guards were quickly knocked out and tied up. The group waited where they were for several minutes to see whether their actions had been noticed by others that were in the courtyard. Nothing changed and so it was assumed that no one noticed.

Two warriors went around the corner and in the door. A moment later, there came the whistle that said all was clear. The rest of the group went around the corner and into the castle in groups of twos and threes. Once they were all inside the door was closed. The cloak that Aldous believed belonged to Tybalt took the lead as they went down the corridor of the castle. This time Aldous knew all the twists and turns that the group was taking.

He knew these halls and he knew what was behind every door that they passed. Aldous could remember all of it as if he had only stepped outside for ten minutes instead of being gone for five years. He had grown up in these hallways and had explored each and every one of them, even the ones his parents had told him that he should not go in to. But that was the point of being a small child, was it not?

The group came to a hallway that went in both directions. Aldous knew which direction they should go, but Tybalt started leading them down the other direction. Aldous stopped and did not move. Several of the warriors stopped as well. Tybalt was aware enough of what was going on that he stopped and turned back. The rest of the group stopped.

"What is it?" Tybalt asked.

"That leads to a guard training room," Aldous said, nodding in the direction that Tybalt had been going, "The other direction leads to the corridor we need to get to the throne room."

"Are you sure?" Tybalt asked. Tybalt was now going over the map in his head.

"This is my castle," Aldous answered, "I know where things are."

"Okay," Tybalt said, "Then we go the other direction." He started off in the direction Aldous had pointed out. The rest of the group fell back into their positions and everyone started following Tybalt, including Aldous.

They followed this hallway to another and then to the main corridor that would take them to the throne room. At one point they could hear the sound of several boots coming down the corridor towards them. Aldous stepped out of his position and opened a door on the left side of the corridor. He went inside and the rest of the group followed him. Tybalt was the last one inside and he closed the door behind him. The room was a storeroom for decorations. Aldous recognized some of them from the costume ball that had been thrown for his father's birthday one year and a set of statues that had been used for decorating the throne room a few weeks before he started the war with Lithimin over Tiregous and the mine.

The boots went passed the door. And when no one could hear the sound of footfalls anymore, Tybalt opened the door and looked out. He waved that it was safe for leaving the room. Everyone followed him out. Aldous closed the door behind them before taking up his position in the middle of the warriors again. They continued down the corridor.

Finally, at the corner just before the main entrance to the throne room Tybalt stopped and everyone following him stopped as well.

"Ready?" Tybalt asked. Cloaked heads nodded. Tybalt and the warriors removed their cloaks and dropped them in a pile near the wall. Each got their weapon out. When Tybalt counted to the three, the warriors, aside from those assigned as bodyguards to Aldous, Casimir, and Alden, went around the corner. Casimir, Alden, Aldous, and their bodyguards stepped out from around the corner a moment afterward. Apparently the group had arrived during a change of the guard. So there were eight guards instead of just four. However, the guards were surprised and overwhelmed. There was enough of a battle to attracted attention. There was a servant farther down the corridor that saw everything. Aldous's bodyguard saw the man and started towards him with his sword in hand. The man dropped the pitcher he had been carrying and ran in the opposite direction. The warrior went back to standing near Aldous. By then the guards were down on the ground and not getting back up. Two warriors opened and held open each door to the throne room. The group had reassembled into the positions laid out by the plan. And the group marched into the throne room.

Garibold and Jarlath were standing at a table on one side of the room. The table was covered with papers and scrolls. Both men looked shocked at the intrusion. And even more surprised at how organized the attack was.

"Who are you?" Garibold demanded. His voice sounded much weaker than Aldous remembered it. Garibold started to move out from behind the table, but Jarlath grabbed his shoulder and held him where he was. Garibold obeyed and stopped moving.

"We are your demise as king," Casimir said. He and Alden removed their hoods and let everyone see their faces.

"It does not work that way," Garibold said.

"There is a treaty in place that prevents you from doing this," Jarlath said, "Unless you are a nation that does not go by their treaties."

"It is not King Casimir that brings the fall of this foolishness," Aldous said. His voice boomed as it used to when he sat on the throne that still sat on the dais.

"And who are you?" Jarlath demanded, though the look on Garibold's face said that he had recognized the voice. Aldous twisted off the clasp that held his cloak on. The cloak fell to the floor, revealing him in his armour and ready for battle.

"You should not be here," Jarlath said.

"What did you think King Casimir would do with me when he received the message that there would be no ransom?" Aldous asked, "It was not likely that he would kill me. And I am not old enough to have died in those five years. And I have been waiting for the chance to take down the man that gave the information of my whereabouts to King Casimir in the first place."

"You will do nothing to me," Jarlath said, "You were a soft king and you will always be known for that weakness."

"That is not a weakness," Aldous said, "That is a choice in caring for the populace of this kingdom. The people you walk over and think nothing of. Those are the people that matter most to a ruler. Because without them there could be no power, no kingdom, no reason for a ruler."

"There will always be peasants that have no place else to go, that beg for the abuse they deserve," Jarlath said.

"The only one in this kingdom that deserves abuse," Aldous said as he started towards where Garibold and Jarlath were standing, "Is you!" Aldous drew his sword. Petrina seemed to gleam with Aldous's anger at Jarlath.

Jarlath pulled out a dagger and grabbed Garibold. He put the dagger against Garibold's shoulder.

"Do not come any closer," Jarlath threatened, "Or I will hurt him."

"Then you will not have a puppet for you to pull the strings of," Aldous replied. He shoved the table out of the way leaving nothing between himself and Jarlath holding Garibold. Garibold seemed frozen and unsure what to do.

"There are others that can play the role of puppet for me," Jarlath said moving the dagger into Garibold's clothing.

"None that are stupid enough to let you rule this kingdom in the way you have been," Aldous said, "Too many people can see what you are doing and the bad effects it is having on this kingdom."

"All you need is to find the right price for the person," Jarlath replied.

"My kingdom is not for sale!" Aldous charged Jarlath. Jarlath pushed the dagger up to its hilt into Garibold's shoulder and Garibold sank to the floor. A moment later Aldous hit Jarlath in the side of his head with the flat side of Petrina. Jarlath was knocked to the ground. Jarlath pulled out another dagger to use on Aldous, but several of Tybalt's warriors restrained him.

They took the dagger away from him and tied him up. Another was looking at the dagger in Garibold's shoulder.

An alarm sounded out in the courtyard to say that the kingdom was under attack. Aldous shook his head. He put Petrina back in to his scabbard and turned back to Casimir. Casimir was standing on the dais near the throne. He was holding the crown in his hands. Everyone was looking at Aldous. Aldous moved to the dais and up the steps. He stood before Casimir. Casimir gently placed the crown on his head then took a step backwards. Another step took him down one of the two steps that led up to the throne. Aldous looked around. He was still the centre of everyone's attention. He sat down on the throne. Casimir bowed as one bows to a king. Alden and Tybalt did so as well. The rest of the warriors went down on one knee as their leaders gave the example. They were all bowing when the first guards arrived in the throne room. The guards saw what was going on. Instead of attacking, they also fell to one knee. Many more filtered in and bowed before Aldous.

Aldous looked out at them. It reminded him of his coronation. He did not really like it then, but he accepted it because it was part of being a king. Once again the feelings appeared that the people should not have to bow to him just because he was born in to this position of power, but the thought itself stopped him. Aldous realized that they were not bowing to him because he had been born in to this role, but because he had earned back the right to sit on this throne and wear this crown. That thought made him straighten up and look over the group with a whole new respect.

"You may rise," Aldous commanded once people had stopped arriving. Everyone looked up at him.

"We have some business," Aldous said his voice booming so that all could hear him, "First of all send a messenger to all our troops and tell them to withdraw and return here."

One of the leaders of the guard picked three men out of the crowd of guards and sent them off after speaking with them for several minutes.

"Next," Aldous said once the men had left the throne room, "Prince Garibold needs a healer. Take him to one, but keep him under guard at all times."

The leader of the guards directed two guards to that task. Aldous watched as they picked up Garibold and left the throne room.

"I want Jarlath to be tied to the pole that is at the top of the tallest tower," Aldous said, "But I do not want him to be killed and anyone that does kill him will suffer my wrath."

The leader of the guard sent four men to do this. The four picked Jarlath up from where he was struggling with the ropes that kept him bound. And they left the room carrying him between the four of them. Aldous doubted that the way they were carrying had anything to do with Jarlath's weight and more to do with inflicting pain.

"This afternoon I want all the records for the crimes and people that have been put in to the dungeon since Prince Garibold took the throne," Aldous said, "In the meantime, I need to speak to the captain of the guard and steward. The rest of you are to go back to what you are suppose to be doing."

Slowly, the throne room emptied until there were two men besides Casimir, Alden, Tybalt and his warriors. They both came close to the dais with some amount of uncertainty. Aldous did not blame their nervousness with all those armed warriors watching them.

"I need rooms made up for my guests," Aldous said, gesturing to the men in the throne room. The steward nodded.

"And I want you to prepare a room for a permanent guest that is a six-year-old boy," Aldous said, "I am taking him in. Also, I want the castle to have the proper amount of servants. Especially remember to get Odoric the baker back in the royal kitchens."

"Your majesty," the steward said, "Many of the servants were drafted into the army."

"I am well aware of that fact," Aldous said, "That is the job of the leader of the guards. He will go through and disband the army. I only want the necessary guards kept. And only those that choose to be in the guard are to be kept."

"Yes, your majesty," the captain of the guard bowed to Aldous.

"You are both dismissed," Aldous said. Both bowed and then left the throne room.

"So, far you are doing a very good job," Casimir said.

"With any luck, I will have this kingdom straightened out by the time I die," Aldous said, "Then my grandchild can take the throne and screw it all up again."

"Your grandchild?" Casimir asked, "I was not aware that Garibold was married."

"He will be," Aldous answered, "Jarlath had that idea right. This kingdom needs an heir, but I already know that I cannot trust Garibold to be able to do it. And I have a servant girl that deserves a reward."

Casimir grinned at that thought.

"I ordered your rooms to be prepared without asking whether you wanted to stay in the castle or whether you were going back to stay with Merchant Zenas," Aldous said.

"And how could we refuse your hospitality?" Casimir asked.

"Wonderful," Aldous got up off the throne and came down the stairs to Casimir. He put his arm around Casimir's shoulders and they started moving forward. "Perhaps you can stay for the feast celebrating my return to the throne. I can guarantee the best bread in the whole kingdom."

Casimir laughed.

# THE TALE IS FINISHED, OR IS IT?

"That sounded like a good adventure tale to tell to your grandchildren," Thompson said, "Who did you hear it from?"

"My grandfather Rory," Mitchell answered, "Though he swore that it was all true."

"My grandmother used to tell me that fairies came to clean her house so that she could spend more time with me," Thompson said, "I believed her until I saw the woman that came in to clean with my own eyes."

"I did not really believe any of it once I was grown," Mitchell said, "But then I was going through the books that were packed away."

"You got space for that library, did you?" Thompson asked.

"And my wife is glad for it," Mitchell answered, "But I found a couple of really old books in the bottom of one of the boxes my grandfather gave me before he died. That was why I called you over here."

"You think I can give you an age for the books?" Thompson asked.

"I was hoping so," Mitchell answered.

"All right, let's see these books," Thompson said. Mitchell opened a box that was sitting on his desk and gently lifted out a book of bound parchment that smelled of really old libraries. It was in very good condition for what Thompson could approximate its age from a distance, but it looked like it had been beaten up back when it was still fairly new. Mitchell offered the book to Thompson, who carefully took it and looked it over.

"It is maybe a couple hundred years old," Thompson said, "Though this type of book is much older." Thompson, with great care, opened the cover and looked at the first page. It read:

*The history of Proster as told by King Aldous the sixth in line after the invasion and destruction of the Batend army.*

In beautiful calligraphy style that was rarely seen in something that was only a couple of hundred-years-old.

"This is impossible," Thompson said, "Unless your grandfather's grandfather was into practical jokes."

"Read the end of it," Mitchell said. Thompson closed the book and shifted it so that he could open the back of the book. The calligraphy style changed, as did the author. Thompson read:

*Garibold trusted a man, whose only vision was of getting power, to advise him in the ways of being a king. Aldous was released from prison by King Casimir of Lithimin. Together Aldous and King Casimir took the throne away from Garibold and Jarlath, the advisor. Aldous took the throne. His first order of business was to force Garibold into marriage as punishment. Aldous had Garibold marry the serving girl, Faye. They produced a son in their third year of marriage. Aldous stayed on the throne until his grandson, Rory, was of age to take the throne and then he abdicated to Rory. Garibold had fallen in love with his wife during their marriage and the union produced three girls that kept Garibold and his wife busy. Aldous disappeared one day when he decided to go for a walk. The whole kingdom was searched but no evidence of his body turned up. Rory ruled the kingdom of Proster for many years.*

*-King Rory, the eighth in line after the invasion and destruction of the Batend army.*

"Children's stories," Thompson said, but his voice betrayed him. He was not as sure of that as he had been even five minutes earlier. Mitchell took the book and carefully placed it back in the box on his desk.

"How old would you guess that the books are?" Mitchell asked.

"There are more?" Thompson asked.

"There are four in total, though I believe Aldous did write five while he was in prison," Mitchell answered, "What happened to the fifth book I do not know."

"But those books could prove everything that we know about history to be wrong," Thompson stood up to face Mitchell.

"That is why I want you to tell me how old you think they are," Mitchell said.

"We should be telling everyone about this discovery," Thompson said.

"They would take the books away from me and burn them as falsehoods and lies," Mitchell said, "Just tell me how old do you think they are."

"A couple hundred years at most," Thompson said.

"Thank you," Mitchell said. Mitchell picked up a handful of dust from the bowl on his desk as Thompson started into the rest of his argument about revealing the books and blew it in to Thompson's face. Thompson's face took on a blank look.

"We spent the afternoon talking about how the library is coming along," Mitchell told Thompson, "You never saw the book of history or remember that I asked you the age of some books. You will not remember that the books even exist."

Thompson's face slowly when back to normal. He looked surprised to find himself standing up.

"What was I about to say?" Thompson asked Mitchell.

"You said that you needed to get going," Mitchell answered.

"Of course," Thompson said, "I am sorry. I do not usually space out like that." Thompson started for the door with Mitchell following him.

"You will have to come back when I am finished," Mitchell said.

"You will probably fill all the shelves and still have more books," Thompson said.

"I will see," Mitchell said. Thompson stepped into the hallway.

"See you," Thompson called back as he headed down the hallway.

"See you," Mitchell called after him and then closed the door. Mitchell went back to his desk. He locked the box that contained the books as well as several of his own journals that the government would not welcome coming to light. Lifting the box he took it to one corner of the library. He put the box on the floor before getting down there himself. He opened a panel in the back of the bookshelf and pushed the box inside. Then he closed the panel. Getting up off the floor, Mitchell dusted himself off before going back to shelving books from an open box.

# ABOUT THE AUTHOR

Heather Mantler is a lover of fairy tales and fables. She is also a student of psychology. She lives in Prince George, British Columbia. Heather is always working on another story and hopes to have more books out soon.

Heather encourages all her readers to post their reviews on amazon.com.